HE'LL DO WHATEVER IT TAKES TO GET BY.

IF YOU WERE TWELVE OR under, you could ride the buses for free in the tri-valley area, even from town to town.

Jayson needed six buses and nearly two hours to do it, but he finally made it to Percy. He thought about going past Percy, but he figured he'd be safe here, it was far enough away from Moreland.

He didn't want anyone to recognize him in the store.

Of course, it only mattered if he made a mistake. So far he hadn't made any mistakes stealing food, hadn't been caught a single time.

On the way to Percy he kept telling himself that this was no different, and no harder, than stealing a loaf of bread or a jar of Jif peanut butter. Telling himself he needed new sneaks to get by. That he'd had plenty of practice taking what he needed by now, that he knew how to do it and get away.

Just pick the right moment. Be cool and do it.

He remembered something Richie once told him: "It's only a crime if you get caught."

Jayson didn't plan on getting caught.

BOOKS BY MIKE LUPICA

Travel Team

Heat

Miracle on 49th Street

Summer Ball

The Big Field

Million-Dollar Throw

The Batboy

Hero

The Underdogs

True Legend

QB 1

Fantasy League

Fast Break

Last Man Out

THE COMEBACK KIDS SERIES:

Hot Hand

Two-Minute Drill

Long Shot

Safe at Home

Shoot-Out

MIKE LUPICA

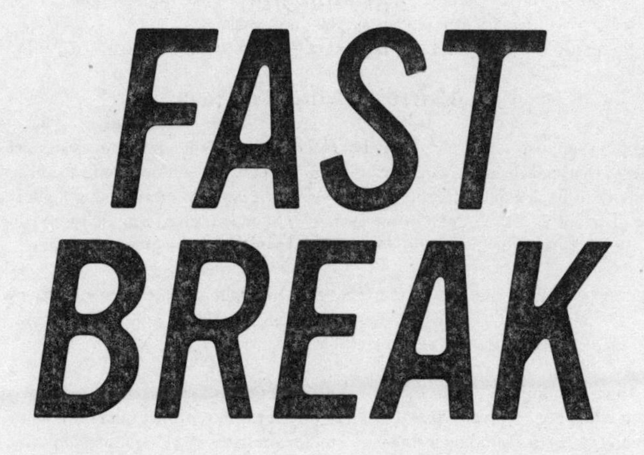

FAST BREAK

PUFFIN BOOKS

PUFFIN BOOKS
An imprint of Penguin Random House LLC
375 Hudson Street
New York, New York 10014

First published in the United States of America by Philomel Books,
an imprint of Penguin Random House LLC, 2015
Published by Puffin Books, an imprint of Penguin Random House LLC, 2016

THE LIBRARY OF CONGRESS HAS CATALOGED THE PHILOMEL BOOKS EDITION AS FOLLOWS:
Lupica, Mike.
Fast break / Mike Lupica.
p. cm.
Summary: Since his mother's death, Jayson, twelve, has focused on basketball and surviving but he is found out and placed with an affluent foster family of a different race, and must learn to accept many changes, including facing his former teammates in a championship game.
ISBN 978-0-399-25606-6 (hc)
[1. Foster home care—Fiction. 2. Basketball—Fiction. 3. Race relations—Fiction.
4. Homeless persons—Fiction. 5. Orphans—Fiction.] I. Title.
PZ7.L97914Fas 2015
[Fic]—dc23
2015003511

Puffin Books ISBN 9781101997833

Edited by Michael Green. Designed by Siobhán Gallagher.

Printed in the United States of America

9 10 8

This book is for the great William Goldman.

1

HIS NAME WAS JAYSON BARNES. But to his friends at school and on the court, he was known as Snap. His friend Tyrese Rice had given him the nickname one time, and it stuck.

"You're like the basketball version of that Snapchat," Ty had said. "One of those pictures you take with your phone and then it's there, but only for a few seconds. Then it's gone." He snapped his fingers. "Gone."

Jayson was all right with that. Sometimes he wanted to make himself disappear for real, from this part of Moreland, North Carolina, growing up this poor. Growing up mad. The guys he balled with at the Jefferson Houses, or the Jeff, as they called it, were always telling him how mad he played, the edge he had to him, the way he'd get into it with somebody on the other team the first time they gave him a shove or tried to get away with something.

It wasn't like he didn't have his reasons.

The Jefferson Houses were part of public housing on the east side of Moreland. There had been just one building at first, between the train tracks and the river, but now there were four: Jefferson, Washington, Adams, Lincoln—yet they were still known as the Jeff. And everybody on both sides of Moreland knew that the court there was where some of the best ball in town was played.

Jayson and his mom had lived at the Jeff until the landlord kicked them out for not paying the rent. They'd had no choice but to move to the Pines, a building even more run-down than the Jeff, practically right on top of the railroad tracks. When the trains would come barreling past, the walls of Jayson's apartment would shake so bad it felt like an earthquake. He was just waiting for the day the entire building would collapse. That's why he kept his basketball trophies in a drawer in his bedroom; he was sure that if he put them on top of his wobbly desk, they would fall and shatter one of these days.

Jayson had been embarrassed to move to the Pines at the time. Now he just wanted things back the way they were there.

These days, Jayson spent as much time as possible on the court at the Jeff. Most of the kids there were black, so Jayson would have stood out anyway, with his pale skin, long hair, and the old floppy socks that bunched up at the top of sneakers he'd grown out of from last year to this. But that wasn't the real reason he stood out. It was the style and flash—and snap—he played with, the tricks he could do with the ball, and his all-around fakery.

Ty once told Jayson that he played blacker than any kid in the game, and faster.

"You ever notice," Ty had been saying on the court just this afternoon, "how no one can ever stay in front of you? Like guarding something already happened."

"Got to be fast to stay ahead," Jayson said, looking at the high-rise buildings around them, the view always the same, wondering, like he did, if he'd have to wait until he finished high school to make his greatest move—getting out of the projects.

"Ahead of what?"

"You know what I mean. Ahead of everyone. Everything."

Ty had nodded like he understood, but he didn't, because even he didn't know Jayson's secret. Jayson loved Tyrese like a brother, but couldn't trust him, because even at twelve Jayson had decided that the only person he could really trust was himself.

So he did what he always did when he felt himself wanting to drop his guard a little, and turned the talk to basketball. Just the night before, the Wizards had beaten LeBron and the Cavs, John Wall and Bradley Beal combining for 65 points. There had been long stretches in the game when you thought neither one of them would ever miss again.

"Ty," Jayson said. "You think I got more John Wall in me, or Beal?"

"Wall," said Tyrese. "A born point guard." He faked a jump shot, his eyes following the imaginary ball as it swished through the net. "Me? I'm Beal, lighting it up from the outside."

Jayson just smiled and nodded.

"That'll be us someday," Ty said. "At Carolina or Duke. You passing, me shooting. Cutting down the nets on the way to the Final Four."

"No doubt," Jayson said, not wanting to tell his best friend that when he was old enough to play college basketball, his plan was to get as far away from North Carolina as possible. Nothing against the state. It seemed like everybody here loved basketball as much as he did.

He just needed to get away from his life, from going to bed hungry, from keeping his hair long because he couldn't afford to go get it cut, from wearing sneakers that shamed him—because sneakers could, in basketball, when they were too old and too dirty and too small.

And his friends wondered why he played mad, why he was always up in somebody's chest.

One time he'd even gotten into it with Shabazz Towson, the best center their age in town and one of his best friends. It had been the last game of the day at the Jeff, Jayson's team up by a basket, needing one more to win by two. He beat his man, got into the lane, twisted his body at the last second to create space with Shabazz, tried to put up a teardrop shot.

Shabazz knocked both Jayson and the shot away.

When he tried to help Jayson up, Jayson slapped his hand away. Then he was right up on Shabazz.

"You got some cheap game in you."

"Hey, man, we're boys, remember?" Shabazz said before Tyrese pulled Jayson away.

"You're on the other team," Jayson replied. "On the court,

you're not my friend."

Went right back to the rim on the next play, pulled the ball down, made a scoop shot to win the game. Then he glared at Shabazz and walked away, Shabazz knowing his friend well enough that it meant nothing, would be forgotten as soon as they left the court.

Jayson was smart enough about himself—smart enough, period—to know it was never just one thing. Being hungry and not being able to afford new kicks, that was only part of it. That was why he spent as much time on the basketball court as possible. Worked on his game as though it was all that mattered.

He knew there were things he could do just because he *could*, thinking that maybe God had given him a gift for playing ball because He had to give Jayson something.

He could dribble past a guy in a blink, put the ball behind his back or cross over with it. Could ball-fake you like he had the ball on a string. His friends told him he made the game look easy. But he knew how much of that came because of how hard he practiced.

He never got tired of practicing. It never bothered him being alone on the court, because even then, the game made him feel less alone.

So he'd picture the move he wanted to make, get it straight in his mind. Then he'd make it happen, sometimes feeling as if it were some kind of replay, because he'd already imagined it. It was the same way when he was getting ready to steal, the way he was now.

See yourself do it first, then be gone in a flash.

Like you disappeared.

But he knew making a steal required more than speed. You had to be smart, you had to pay attention, you had to pick your spot, pick the exact right moment to make your move.

Mostly what you had to do was watch their eyes, make sure your concentration was working for you the moment they lost theirs.

That's when you had them.

It wasn't just the element of surprise, Jayson knew, even though it was nice to have that going for you. No, as good as surprise was, acting cool was even better. The best kind of move was the one they didn't expect. You had to let them think they were in control of the moment, when it was really you calling the play all along.

Jayson was almost there right now.

Waiting for him to turn his head, to take his eyes off Jayson just long enough.

Wait for it.

Jayson's face the picture of calm, showing nothing.

Now.

The man behind the counter, Mr. Karlini, turned his head. Jayson, using those quick hands, put the loaf of bread under his sweatshirt. Then he walked calmly toward the door of the Broad Avenue Food Mart like he had all the time in the world, Mr. Karlini still talking to the old woman who'd come in at just the right moment to buy a lottery ticket.

Jayson still wasn't taking any chances, didn't want Mr. Karlini to look over and maybe spot the bulge in the front of his old Duke sweatshirt. So he angled his body just slightly away from him, trying not to be obvious about it.

He hadn't been back to this store in a week, not since he stole the jar of peanut butter. Jayson tried not to hit the same store twice in the same week; he didn't want guys like Mr. Karlini to get suspicious since he never actually bought anything.

Jayson kept walking at his normal pace, slowing down when he got near the magazine rack, stopping to look at the cover of *HOOP.*

"Something in particular you were looking for?" Mr. Karlini said, startling him a little. But Mr. Karlini was smiling. "Snap, isn't that what your friends call you?"

"Nah, I was just hanging, Mr. Karlini, waiting for my friend. Guess he forgot me."

"Well, you have a nice day."

"You too."

It bothered him a little when they were nice to him, and Mr. Karlini was maybe the nicest of all. But Jayson was out of bread and nearly out of peanut butter, and he was hungry. Every day he tried to fill up as much as he could on lunch in the cafeteria at Moreland East Middle. But then he'd get to playing ball and by the time he went home, his stomach felt so empty it was as if he'd never eaten at all.

The best nights were when Ty or Shabazz would invite him

over for dinner, neither one of them ever saying anything about why they never got invited to Jayson's. But that didn't happen too often, especially on school nights.

The rest of the time, Jayson was on his own, something he had grown used to.

This was the way it had been since his mother had died and her last boyfriend, Richie, had up and left about a week later. None of his friends knew. Not about any of it. They just thought Jayson and his mom had moved to the Pines because they couldn't afford the Jeff anymore, and that nobody had seen her lately because she was sick.

In truth, no one other than Jayson and Richie had even noticed his mom much when she was alive. Not for the last couple years of her life, at least. It was like she had already disappeared.

"I don't think it was the drinking or the drugs that killed her," Richie had told him. "I think she died from being sad."

Jayson didn't disagree, though he knew that the drinking and the drugs hadn't helped. Anyway, the why of his mom's death didn't matter much in the end. The point was, his mom was gone. Then Richie was gone.

Only Jayson remained in the apartment at the Pines. And Jayson wasn't about to let that change.

For now, Jayson was managing, stealing just enough to eat, trying not to think about what would happen now that there was no money left to pay the bills.

So far, nobody from Child Protective Services had come

knocking at his door, but he knew it was only a matter of time before he got caught. A teacher was going to figure it out. Or Ty's mother, or his coach at school, or somebody else. And then Jayson would either have to run faster than he ever had on a basketball court, or go into the foster care system.

The apartment may not have been much, not with his mother gone, but it was the only home he knew. Along with the basketball court at the Jeff.

He ran in that direction now, across Third Street, across Fourth, heading east on Broad, taking the bread out from under his blue sweatshirt, putting it in his right hand, pretending it was a basketball, pumping his hand up and down, air-dribbling it.

Jayson (Snap) Barnes was flying now. There one second. Gone the next.

2

THE BEST THING YOU COULD say about Richie Keegan was this: He wasn't nearly as bad as some of the others his mom had brought around. But then, his mom had always thought that the next guy in her life was going to be the one who would provide her and Jayson the better life she said they both deserved.

Jayson knew his mom had loved him. And he had loved her. He knew how hard it was for her to raise him alone, before the drinking and the pills—and whatever else she was using when he wasn't around to see—just seemed to swallow her up. When Jayson had been old enough to ask about his father, all she'd told him was this:

"He was the first one who left."

Jayson knew she had gone through all kinds of jobs when she was still able to work, before she just finally gave up, from hairdresser to waitress to housekeeper, until her real job seemed to become "going from one Richie to another." Jayson knew she was always trying to get clean, going to her AA meetings, promising him that she was going to be a better person and a better mother, that she owed that to her little boy.

And he knew she always meant it. Even when she was making another mess in her life or trying to clean one up, as one man after another would leave her and make her sad, she was somehow still there every day when Jayson would come home from school or from playing ball. Jayson knew she didn't love herself very much. But he knew she loved him and wanted to do better for him. She just didn't know how.

Instead, she just seemed to get older and sicker. And so sad she essentially disappeared, never even leaving their run-down apartment.

It was late summer when Debbie Barnes died. Jayson had just started seventh grade.

With his mom gone, Jayson knew it wouldn't be long before Richie left him too. At least Richie had scraped up enough money to bury his mother. An old friend of his worked at a small cemetery in Kirkville, about a half hour away. Richie threw the guy some money so they didn't have to register the death, which Richie said would have had all kinds of people asking questions about what had happened to Debbie Barnes's twelve-year-old boy.

They buried her one night in a cheap pine box. Jayson had asked Richie to put one of his trophies in with her. He remembered Richie saying some kind of prayer. All Jayson did was say goodbye. Then the two of them left Richie's friend from the cemetery to do his job, Jayson knowing he was never coming back there.

Not long after came the night when Richie had shaken Jayson awake, his duffel bag packed and sitting at the end of Jayson's bed, and told him he had to leave town.

"Like when?" Jayson said.

"Like now."

"When are you coming back?"

"I'm not, kid. Keep your head low or you'll end up in the foster care system."

Richie said he didn't have much time, so Jayson had to listen up. He said he'd paid two months of the electric bill and a month of rent. They also had another month's rent on deposit.

And that was it. Richie shook Jayson's hand and walked out the door, Jayson thinking at the time that at least Richie would be the last guy ever to leave his mom.

3

JAYSON WAS NEVER THE BEST student. He was plenty smart enough, but school just wasn't his thing.

Until this year, at least. It wasn't some new teacher or subject that made Jayson so excited about seventh grade at Moreland East Middle School—it was basketball. There was a new competition for middle school teams all across the state—public and private schools included. If you won the league tournament at the end of your regular season, you got a chance to play in the county tournament. If you won *that*, you got a chance to compete in the first-ever middle-grade basketball championship in the basketball-crazed state of North Carolina. The best part? The finals would be played at Cameron Indoor Stadium—the home of the Duke Blue Devils.

So their coach, Mr. Rankin, had asked the kids he'd picked for the team to focus on school ball this year instead of rec ball or AAU ball. Jayson had gone along.

"This new league is going to be a huge deal," Coach Rankin had told the guys, "and I think if we make it to the states, it would be the best chance for you to shine, and for people to see you, including from prep schools all up and down the East Coast.

"Plus, Cameron Indoor! Doesn't get better than that in college ball. Might as well check the place out before you play there for real someday," Mr. Rankin had said, smiling at Jayson.

In my dreams, Jayson had thought.

There were four teams in the new league from Moreland: Moreland East; Moreland West; St. Patrick's, which was a Catholic school; and Belmont Country Day, a private school on the west side of town in the area known as the Hills. Jayson knew all the teams were going to be good, because he'd played against most of the guys on the other teams in rec leagues. There were eight teams in the league, total.

But Jayson knew something else.

The Moreland East Mavericks were loaded, and not just because they had Jayson and Tyrese in the backcourt. They also had Shabazz, who was already 5'10" He looked even skinnier than Jayson, just because he was so much taller, but he was strong, could shoot and pass, and run the court. According to Shabazz, his family doctor said he might grow another foot before he was through. For now, though, Shabazz being 5'10" was just fine for Jayson. Jayson had somebody who could keep up with him on the break even when Shabazz was the one who'd start the break with a rebound and outlet pass. And Shabazz was somebody who already understood, just from playing with Jayson so much last season, how they could both make a living off the high pick-and-roll.

In addition to Shabazz, Ty, and Jayson, the Mavericks had

Paul Henderson at power forward, and Raymond Bretton at small forward, who was maybe the best pure shooter on the team. Terry Thompson was their first player off the bench; he could play small forward or come in for Tyrese at shooting guard.

Right before the team's first practice, Mr. Rankin passed out their jerseys. He gave Jayson the first pick, his teammates all knowing he would go with number 3, Chris Paul's number, Paul being his favorite player. Tyrese then took number 4, saying that he wanted that one so nothing could come between him and Jayson, not even a number.

After each player had a uniform number, it was time to play. Then it was like all the other basketball days and nights in Jayson's life. For a little while he wouldn't be tired or hungry or worried about money or Child Protective Services or having to forge his mom's name on homework papers.

For the next two hours, he was in charge of the world. He was the one with the ball in his hands, the one who could make things happen the way he wanted them to. It was another day when nobody could get in front of him, or stop him.

He ran the court on a fast break and kicked it to Tyrese in the places on the wing that Ty liked to call his sweet spots. He lobbed passes to Shabazz and put the ball on the floor and drove into the paint against Ricky Moore, the backup point guard, getting to the rim whenever he wanted to.

And like always he played mad, showing mercy for no one. He loved attacking the second-teamers in particular, telling himself it wasn't his job to make them look like first-stringers; that was their job. If he could embarrass them, he would.

Jayson never doubted he was a good teammate. He knew guys had always wanted to play on his team, not just because of the way he passed the ball, but because he gave them the best chance to win. In his mind, though, the only teammates who mattered were the four he was on the court with at any given moment.

Someday, basketball was going to be his ticket out of this town, and not in the middle of the night, the way it had been for Richie.

It was a good, hard practice today, the first team looking as if they didn't just want to make it to Cameron Indoor, but wanted to try their luck playing the Duke Blue Devils when they got there. When it was over, the guys split up to shoot free throws, and Coach Rankin called Jayson over.

"I see you've been working on your left hand," Coach Rankin said.

"I work on my whole game, all the time," Jayson said, the words having a little bite to them.

"You know, it wouldn't kill you to smile once in a while out there," Coach said. "Let your teammates see that basketball makes you as happy as it does them."

"It *does* make me happy." Even Jayson heard the edge in his voice.

Coach nodded, a smile on his face that Jayson couldn't quite read. Then he looked down at Jayson's sneakers: dirty low-cut Nikes that Jayson had already grown out of. He'd had to cut a small hole for his right big toe. Sometimes he'd have to soak his feet at night from running around all day in basketball shoes that were at least a size too small.

"Everything good at home?" Coach asked.

"Never better." Jayson forced a smile.

"Still saving up for new sneakers for the season?"

"I'll have 'em by next week," Jayson said. "Just waiting for the right time to go shopping with my mom. Got my eyes on some Zooms, blue-and-white, like our colors. And same color as the Blue Devils, perfect for when we walk onto the court at Cameron Indoor."

The last part was true, at least. The Zooms. The colors.

"Can't wait to see them," Coach said. "Now go knock down some free throws with the guys."

Jayson did, taking his turn with Ty and Shabazz, doing what he always did, pretending he had to make the next two to win the game. When they were done shooting, he looked around the gym, saw his teammates, saw them laughing and chasing down balls, still felt all the life in the place even with practice winding down.

This had always been the best time of the year for Jayson, no matter what was going on at home. Just having a team around him, like his basketball family was his real family, like the gym was his own safe place.

But Jayson was feeling out of place now.

He might've been the best player out there, might even have been the best twelve-year-old player in the county. Yet he was also the only player who couldn't afford a pair of new basketball *shoes*.

4

IF YOU WERE TWELVE OR under, you could ride the buses for free in the tri-valley area, even from town to town.

Jayson needed six buses and nearly two hours to do it, but he finally made it to Percy. He thought about going past Percy, but he figured he'd be safe here, it was far enough away from Moreland.

He didn't want anyone to recognize him in the store.

Of course, it only mattered if he made a mistake. So far he hadn't made any mistakes stealing food, hadn't been caught a single time.

On the way to Percy he kept telling himself that this was no different, and no harder, than stealing a loaf of bread or a jar of Jif peanut butter. Telling himself he needed new sneaks to get by. That he'd had plenty of practice taking what he needed by now, that he knew how to do it and get away.

Just pick the right moment. Be cool and do it.

He remembered something Richie once told him: "It's only a crime if you get caught."

Jayson didn't plan on getting caught.

The store he'd picked out was a Foot Locker in the middle of downtown Percy, a Starbucks on one side of it, a Dunkin' Donuts across the street. He figured they must like their coffee here. He'd gotten off at a bus stop two blocks away on Main Street. The bus stop was next to a small white church, and Jayson could see a playground with a hoop and what looked like a half-court behind the church. He noticed that the hoop had a net attached to it. *Nice.*

Nothing in this town reminded him of the Pines.

He walked up and down Main Street for a while, his eyes taking everything in at once the way they did when he was playing a game, looking at the players in front of him. The steeple on the church, women pushing baby strollers, people smiling at each other, looking happy. He wondered what it would be like to have this world be his world, have this town be his town.

He passed a kid his age on the street and wondered what there was to be afraid of in Percy, knowing it couldn't be something as simple as a knock on the door.

He had worn an old, beat-up pair of black sliders, with socks, knowing how geeked-out socks made you look when you wore them with a pair of flip-flops. But he knew that when he made it out of the Foot Locker with his new sneakers, he didn't want to be leaving his old Kobes behind. Even though they were too small, he was going to use them until they fell apart, and didn't want to wear his new ones outside on concrete until he absolutely had to.

You needed two pairs of sneakers, even if you had to steal one of them.

Finally he stood outside the Foot Locker, across the street, watching the people go in and out. Kids going in with a parent, sometimes two, then coming out later carrying bags. Sometimes the kids were already wearing their new shoes; Jayson recognized the newness of them all the way across the street, trying to remember what that new-shoe feel was really like.

He took a deep breath and walked across the street and through the front door, feeling a little bit like he did when a game was about to begin.

He told himself to keep thinking like that, keep telling himself this was just a game. It was easy, the stuff you could convince yourself of when you wanted, the lies you could tell yourself. So Jayson, all the way over here and through all the waiting, had convinced himself that Foot Locker wasn't going out of business if they got shorted the cost of one pair of new kicks. No one would even notice.

There was a lot going on inside the store, all these salespeople wearing their black-and-white striped shirts. They seemed to be moving every which way, running to get boxes of sneakers, talking to customers, some of them wearing little headsets with microphones attached. Music blared with a thumping bass. And, luckily, there were no security scanners by the door. Right away Jayson knew he'd gotten lucky, that by accident he'd picked the perfect store.

"Something I can help you with?" a voice behind him said, over the music, startling him.

He turned around and saw a tall, skinny, smiling black kid in one of those striped ref shirts. The badge in front said "De'Ron."

"Just looking."

"Well, if you need help finding anything, give me a shout," De'Ron said. "And, dude, I do mean *shout*," he added with a smile.

"Thanks."

Jayson wasn't ready yet. So he walked along the walls, where all the sneakers were displayed by brand, some of them costing as much as $200.

He realized after a while that he was spending as much time checking out the kids in here and their parents as he was the rows of shoes in front of him, watching them talk and laugh and point, all of them just having a normal Saturday afternoon, just living their lives.

Jayson thought, *And I'm living mine.*

He finally caught De'Ron's eye and gave him the nod, took him over and showed him the Zooms, told him his size. Then, because he'd planned it out this way, he also asked for some Mad Handle 2s, slightly more expensive, same size.

"Might end up spending all my birthday money today," Jayson said, giving De'Ron a fake smile.

He sat down, waited for De'Ron to come back with both boxes, and tried on the Mad Handle 2s first. He took his time lacing them up, hoping that De'Ron would go help somebody else, a *paying* customer, and maybe even forget that Jayson was here.

"How those feel?" De'Ron said when Jayson had both of them on.

"Real sweet," Jayson said. "Now let's try the others." Then he went through the same slow process with the Zooms.

"How those feel?" De'Ron said.

"Just as sweet."

"Walk around on them a little bit to make sure."

Jayson made sure not to walk toward the door; he walked toward the back of the store instead. It felt even more crowded in here now than when he first came in. Even the music seemed louder. Jayson gave one quick look back, saw De'Ron talking to another customer, smiling and nodding, and told himself that he couldn't feel bad here the way he did when he was stealing food from Mr. Karlini's store. Told himself that he was just doing what he had to do to survive. That he needed basketball to survive as much as he needed food.

He waited until he caught De'Ron's eye, gave him another fake smile, came back to where he'd been sitting.

"I'm not sure. They're a little bit tight now that I walk in them. I'd better try the Handles on one more time," Jayson said. "Somebody told me once, if they don't fit in the store, they'll never fit. And, you know, they've got to be *just right*."

"Tell me about it. You a player?"

"Yeah."

"Whereabouts?"

"Akersville."

Lying really was like ball. More you did it, better you got at it.

Jayson tried the Adidas back on, shook his head, put the Zooms on, and frowned. De'Ron seemed to be losing interest; there were other people waiting to be helped.

"Can I try the next half-size up?" Jayson asked. "Just so I can make sure?"

"Lemme make sure we've got them," De'Ron said.

Now De'Ron was the one walking toward the back of the store. Jayson turned and looked at the front door, saw a man and woman about to come through it with their daughter.

Now.

This was like an opening in a game, the daylight you got between defenders, one that opened fast and closed even faster.

He walked toward the exit, telling himself not to hurry, and held the door open for the little girl. The mom said, "Well, thank you! Maybe manners aren't dead in our little town after all."

"You're welcome." Jayson kept his head down and waited for the whole family to enter, then calmly walked out the door, like he was on the court, using them as a screen.

Not even breathing now.

He'd scoped out Main Street before entering the store, knew that the closest side street was to his left when he got out on the sidewalk. He'd seen that there was a pretty long block once you turned the corner, with more side streets splitting off from there.

Jayson walked left, heart pounding, still telling himself not to hurry when what he really wanted to do was run. The one thing he'd stopped to do once he got outside was pull down his sweatpants so they'd cover the white of the new sneakers, which he imagined were brighter than headlights on a car.

Once he made the left at the corner, *then* he was going to run, to use his speed when he needed it the most.

Almost there.

That's when he felt a large hand clamp down on his shoulder.

"Where do you think you're going, son?" a man's voice said.

Jayson turned around to find a tall white-haired man. He wasn't wearing a striped shirt, just a short-sleeved one that said "Foot Locker" on the front, and underneath that, "Manager."

"I was just looking for my mom," Jayson said. "She was supposed to meet me here."

"Look at me," the man said.

Jayson looked up.

"Don't lie to me," the man said.

"It's the truth!" Jayson said.

"Don't make it worse, son."

Staring at him now.

"Do I know you?"

Jayson looked back down. "No."

"Wait . . . I *do* know you. My team played a game against

you in summer ball over in Moreland last year. Nobody forgets a kid who can play like you."

Jayson had nothing to say to that.

"We're going to take a walk back to the store now," the man said. "And when we get there, we do need to find your mom and figure out what to do about those sneakers you just tried to steal."

Jayson thought about breaking loose, making a run for it. But it was too late for that, especially now that the man knew who he was.

The man kept his hand on Jayson's shoulder as they walked back down Main Street. Jayson told himself he wasn't going to cry in front of this man, even though he felt like crying for the first time since they put his mom in the ground.

He walked toward the store and knew in his heart that he was being walked right into the Child Protective Services system. He didn't know how it worked or where he was going, but he was smart enough to know that the game was officially over.

5

THE SOCIAL WORKER, MS. MORETTI, sat across the desk from Jayson.

They were in her office in Moreland's town hall, on Broad Avenue, early Saturday night. It had been a few hours since Jayson had tried to steal the sneakers, but it seemed like everything that had happened since had happened fast.

None of it had been good.

The store manager, who'd told Jayson to call him Pete, like they were buddies, had asked him a lot of the same questions Ms. Moretti was asking him now. "How old are you?" "Where are your parents?" "Where do you live and who do you live *with*?"

Pete had eventually called the Moreland police and told them what happened. He offered to drive Jayson over to Moreland himself, but the policeman said that's not the way it worked. An officer would pick Jayson up and drive him to the Child Protective Services office at the town hall, and a social worker would meet them there.

The social worker turned out to be Ms. Moretti. She had long red hair and glasses on top of her head. She went over every detail of his life, asking every question twice, making sure she felt Jayson was telling her the truth.

"You said your mom passed away last month?"

"She didn't pass away," he said. "She died."

"And you don't know where your father is."

"I don't know *who* my father is."

"You never even had a name?"

"Jamie."

"No last name?"

Jayson shook his head.

"Do you know if he still lives in North Carolina?"

"I asked my mom one time where he was and she said, 'A bar.'"

"So you never had any contact with him?"

Jayson shook his head and looked out the window, the lights of Moreland coming on. It occurred to him that he was only a few blocks away from Mr. Karlini's store, where he'd convinced himself he was so good at stealing food that he could steal a pair of basketball shoes without getting caught.

"And after your mom died, you lived with her friend Richie until he left?"

"I told the man at the store all of this already, and then the police when they asked me."

"Jayson?" she said in a soft voice. "I'm not them. I'm trying to help you."

"Then let me go. I'll earn the money and pay the man back for the shoes, swear."

"We're past that," she said. "You understand that, right?"

He nodded.

"You've been living by yourself since Richie left. Weren't you afraid?"

"Just of ending up here."

"You're telling me that nobody in your building knew a twelve-year-old boy was living by himself?"

Jayson shook his head. "We never got to really know anyone else at the Pines."

"And your friends? Nobody asked about your mom?"

"If they had, I would've told them she was sick but getting better."

"What about your teachers?"

"If you do good enough at school, they leave you alone. Richie signed my papers once before he left. I've been doing it since then."

"A seventh grader living on his own. No one noticed. That's sad."

Jayson just shrugged.

"What were you doing for food?"

Jayson stared at the floor. "I stole."

Ms. Moretti took her glasses off her head and put them on, like she needed something to do with her hands while she thought of what she wanted to say next. Jayson could see the pity in her eyes.

"I don't need you feeling sorry for me," he said. "I'm all right."

"You are? How can that be?" she said in a soft voice.

"I'm not, actually," Jayson said. "I'm hungry."

She said she could do something about that, and asked him what he liked on his pizza.

"Pepperoni," he said.

Ms. Moretti nodded.

"And sausage," Jayson added.

She smiled. "And sausage."

After she called in the order, she said, "You mind if I ask one more question, just for now?"

Jayson sighed. "You're going to ask it no matter what I say."

"What were you going to do when you couldn't pay the rent or the bills?"

Just like that, he wanted to cry. He could feel the tears coming, knew he was too tired to fight them back. But he tried, using anger like he always did.

"I don't know!" he yelled across the desk. "Okay? I can't answer the questions you're asking me!"

Ms. Moretti was silent. Jayson expected her to get angry back. Instead, she reached out her hand toward his and said, "Okay."

That's when Jayson lost his fight against the tears.

They ate the pizza in silence at her desk, Ms. Moretti giving Jayson a cold Snapple from the refrigerator in her office to go with it. The pizza was good, and still hot when the kid brought it.

When they finished eating, Jayson looked at Ms. Moretti and said, "What happens now?"

She said, "I make some calls."

"To who?"

"To the potential foster care parents on my list."

"To see if any of *them* want to take pity on me?"

"To see if any of them want to help you get the life you deserve," she answered.

Then: "Would you mind sitting in my outer office for a few minutes?"

"Do I have a choice?"

"The choice you're about to make is about a better life," she said.

"Who says I won't run away once I'm out of here?"

"No one. And if you did, I don't think I could catch you, even though I played some high school basketball myself," she said. "But the two policemen out front probably can."

He shrugged. "Whatever."

"I think there are some copies of *Sports Illustrated* out there."

"Awesome," he said sarcastically.

Truthfully, he was too tired to bolt, but he didn't tell her that. The boy who never seemed to get tired on a basketball court, who was always going at full speed when the other guys in the game were starting to slow down, was tired now. Or beat. Or beaten down. He couldn't decide which. He just thought he could go to sleep right now, without even knowing where he'd end up tonight.

He took a seat in one of the chairs outside and closed his eyes. After about ten minutes Ms. Moretti came out of her office and said, "Well, that didn't take long."

"Awesome," he said again.

He didn't believe for a second that she'd really found someone who would want him. Ms. Moretti had probably offered them money or something.

"It took only one phone call, to the Lawtons, first names on my list."

"Why would they want me to live with them when they haven't even met me?"

"I told them about you."

"And they still want me? Are they *stupid*?"

She ignored that, shut off the lights in her office, shut the door behind her.

"Why don't we go meet them and you can decide for yourself?" She smiled. "Maybe it really will be awesome."

They went down to the lobby of the building. She hadn't been lying about the policemen; the same ones who'd driven him here were sitting in their car out front. Ms. Moretti knocked on the window and said she could take it from here.

"My car's just around the corner," she said, and led the way down Broad Avenue.

One last time, Jayson thought about making a run for it. No way she'd ever be able to catch him, even with him wearing the flip-flops he'd tried to leave behind at the Foot Locker.

But then he thought:

Where would I go?

It was one more thing he'd have to figure out, just not tonight. Tonight he'd let the social worker woman take him home, wherever home was, at least for now.

THEIR NAMES, MS. MORETTI TOLD him on the ride over, were Tom and Carol Lawton. He was a doctor at Moreland Memorial, an orthopedic surgeon.

"Like a sports doctor?"

"Yep—like that," Ms. Moretti said, and then told him Carol Lawton had once been an art history professor at the University of North Carolina before retiring.

They lived in a big house at the end of a street filled with other big houses on the west side of Moreland. The street was lined with enormous trees. It looked like practically every light in the Lawtons' house was on as Ms. Moretti drove up the long driveway. There were two SUVs parked in front of a garage that was bigger than Jayson's apartment at the Pines.

This wasn't just the other side of town. To Jayson, this was like a whole other world.

He knew, even before Ms. Moretti rang the doorbell, just from standing on the front porch with two wicker chairs facing the street, that this was the nicest house he'd ever seen in real life.

Somehow, the day that had started with all those bus rides

over to Percy had brought him here. Him and his social worker.

He hadn't said one word to her once they'd left her office. She tried different ways to start the conversation back up, even asking him questions about basketball and his team. But she finally gave up, like she'd grown tired of having her shot blocked.

The front door opened.

He whispered to Ms. Moretti, "Why didn't you tell me that they were black?"

"You didn't ask me," she said. "Does it make a difference?"

"I just didn't know."

"What? That they had black people on this side of town, or that they lived in houses like this?"

"Both, I guess," he said.

Mr. Lawton was tall, six feet easy. Mrs. Lawton was almost as tall, with lighter skin. The same kind of light-skinned black as Shabazz, whose father was white. She was young-looking, Jayson thought, for someone who had retired.

"Thank you for doing this on such short notice," Ms. Moretti said.

"Kate," Mrs. Lawton said, "if we didn't want to get the call, we wouldn't have our names on your list."

Then she turned and said, "You must be Jayson."

Jayson took a better look at her, another woman smiling at him, putting out her hand for him to shake. He thought about leaving her hanging, but what was the point? What was the point of any of this, ending up here, just because of a pair of stupid sneakers?

He gave her a quick handshake and said, "Yeah."

"You seemed surprised when you saw us standing in the doorway."

"You're black," he said.

It made her laugh, even though he wasn't trying to be funny. She looked at her husband, then back down at herself, and said, "I guess we are!"

Jayson felt the heat rushing to his face. He squared up his shoulders and said, "You making fun of me?"

Ms. Moretti, something hard in her voice for the first time, said, "Be nice, Jayson."

Then they all stood there until Mrs. Lawton said, "Please come in."

She showed them into the living room. There was a fire going. Jayson saw pictures on the mantel above it, the Lawtons with a boy who was taller than both of them, wearing a basketball uniform. It surprised him for some reason. He'd had this idea in his head that people wanted to be foster parents because they didn't have kids of their own.

Jayson sat down next to Kate Moretti on a couch, the Lawtons across from them on another couch that looked exactly the same, a coffee table in between them.

"Can I get something for you, Jayson?" Mrs. Lawton said. "Something to drink, maybe?"

"I'm good."

"Are you sure?"

"I said I'm good."

There was another awkward silence, like the one at the

front door. Everybody except Jayson smiling at everybody else. But he wasn't going to make this easy for them. He didn't care whether they wanted him to be here or not.

He didn't want to be here.

"Why don't we do this for now?" Mrs. Lawton said. "Tom and Kate, why don't you go over some of the details about how we're going to proceed while I go show Jayson his room?"

She stood up. Jayson didn't move, staring down at his hands clenched together in his lap. When he looked up again, he said, "How do you know if you want me to stay? You don't know anything about me."

"Maybe I do," Carol Lawton said.

"You don't know me. You just think I'm some kid likes to steal."

"You don't know what I think, Jayson. But I do know more about you than you realize. You grew up in the Jeff, is that right?"

He was back to staring down at his hands: already big enough to palm a basketball even though he was only twelve, but right now he was using them to hold himself together. "Yeah," he said, "living the dream. You think knowing that makes us close?"

"I grew up about two blocks from there," she said. "Same neighborhood. Same world."

Before he could reply, she added, "But I like it better here. Before you decide you don't, let's at least have a look at what's going to be your bedroom."

Jayson said, "So you think you know me because you come from the east side? You're not anything like me."

"Maybe more than you think," she said.

"Think whatever you want."

"We just met five minutes ago," she said, "so let's agree that I don't know you and you don't know me. At least not yet."

Then she walked toward the stairs he'd seen in the front hall. Jayson followed her, his flip-flop sliders making loud slipping noises on the bare wood floor.

"Jayson," Mrs. Lawton said, "Ms. Moretti told us quite a bit about you on the phone. If I don't know you yet, at least I know something about your life, and how it brought you to us tonight. And I feel like I have at least a little bit of an understanding about your life because we come from the same place. Most of my friends lived in the original Jefferson House. When it was just one building. The Pines hadn't been built yet."

"Awesome," he said. "Thanks for the history lesson."

"And what I believe . . . no, what I'm *sure* of is that if you can survive living on your own at a place like the Pines, you're certainly going to be able to survive living with Tom and me, if that's what you choose."

Jayson laughed. "So now I get to choose?"

"We're not going to force you to stay," she said.

They were at the top of the stairs, walking down a hallway.

"I don't need another mom," he said, the words just spilling out of him.

"I won't try to be your mom."

"Then why do they call you guys foster parents?" he said.

"What are you trying to do? Couldn't you find someone who *wants* to live with you?"

"My husband and I are trying to give you a safe place. And this is a safe place for you, whether you want to believe that or not."

"And you're saying that if I want to leave, I can leave?"

"I hope you're not going to want to leave."

"But you don't know that."

"No." She smiled again. "I don't. The truth. Just an old east side girl talking to an east side boy."

"Old is right." The edge strong in Jayson's voice.

"Jayson," she said. "This is a good place to stop running. But it's up to you to give it a chance."

She said it in the same calm voice she'd been using all along, maybe so it wouldn't sound as if she were arguing with him.

It was the same with her as it was with Ms. Moretti: She was just trying to be nice. But what neither one of them realized was that Jayson didn't *want* them acting all nice. This wasn't his home.

When they reached the bedroom, it only made Jayson more sure. It was bigger than the whole living room at the Pines, with a bed twice as big as his own, a neatly placed blue bedspread on it. There was a large dresser, next to it a TV on a stand. There was a beautiful desk. Through another open door he saw a bathroom.

"What do you think?" she said.

"I think it's a bedroom."

"It's going to be *your* room," she said. "Unless you're even more stubborn than I think."

He went over and sat on the bed, feeling how soft it was underneath him.

"This is really my room now?"

Mrs. Lawton smiled. "It is."

"Then could you please get out of here and leave me alone?"

HE WOKE UP IN HIS new room, in his new house, on Sunday morning, not knowing where he was at first because of how quiet it was.

There was no loud rap music from across the hall, nobody yelling at each other in the apartment upstairs, nobody banging pots and pans next door. At the Pines, where the walls were as thin as tissue paper, you heard everyone's business.

When Jayson opened his eyes and checked the iPhone docked on the nightstand next to him, he realized he had slept until ten o'clock. Maybe it was because this was the best, softest bed he'd ever slept in in his life: big, soft pillows and blankets, like you could pull the quiet up over your head.

He took a shower and got dressed in the same clothes he'd worn yesterday. He took another look around the room, at the strangeness of it all. He picked up one of the soft pillows, held it to his chest. Then he swung it as hard as he could at the iPhone, the whole docking station flying off the table, the phone clattering to the ground and bouncing against a wall.

He went downstairs and found Mr. and Mrs. Lawton

waiting to have breakfast with him, the two of them sitting at the table with their coffee. Mrs. Lawton was reading a book while her husband was reading the sports section of a newspaper.

"How'd you sleep?" Mr. Lawton asked, peering around the newspaper.

"Okay."

Mrs. Lawton gave him that smile of hers. "Must have been more than okay if you're just coming for breakfast now."

"Took me forever to get to sleep," he said, knowing that was a lie. Even with his head spinning over everything that had happened to him, he was gone the moment his head hit the soft pillows, like somebody had knocked him out.

They ate scrambled eggs, bacon, and English muffins, washed down with orange juice. Jayson shoveled in a few bites, head down, not remembering when he had ever eaten like this in the morning.

Jayson's hand gripped the fork and squeezed, forcing himself to slow down, the feel of the metal solid in his hands. He took a deep breath and dropped the fork on his plate, the sound surprising all of them.

"Are you done already?" Mrs. Lawton asked.

"Not hungry," Jayson said.

Mr. Lawton's eyebrows rose, but he didn't say anything.

"All right, then. Suit yourself. The dishes go by the sink. We'll be leaving at noon," Mrs. Lawton said.

"Where to?"

"To buy you some new clothes. You'll be going to school from now on at Belmont Country Day. They have a dress code."

"I'm not going to any school where I have to wear some stupid tie."

"No ties," Mrs. Lawton said. "Just a collared shirt and khaki pants."

"I don't own any khakis."

"Why we're going shopping."

"Why do I even have to go to Belmont?" he said. "Why can't I just stay at Moreland East?"

"You don't live on the east side anymore. You live here."

"Everybody I know is at Moreland East," he said.

It was settling in on him—crushing him—what this all meant. A new house and a new school also meant a new team, and a new coach. He wouldn't be playing in the same backcourt with Tyrese anymore; he wouldn't be dishing to Shabazz. He was going to be playing with a bunch of white-breads who came to school in their nice shirts and their nice pants.

"It will be better for you to get a fresh start," she said.

"At a school where I won't know anybody."

"You'll make new friends," she said.

"I had all the friends I needed where I was."

"You needed a lot more than friends. Give the school a chance like I hope you'll give us a chance."

"Because that's what's you want?"

"Because it's what *you* will want."

Jayson said, "You know why it wasn't so bad living on my

own? Because I got to decide what was best for me, or what I wanted to wear. Or who my friends were."

"You also didn't have anybody who cared enough about you to tell you that you didn't have to be mad at the world all the time."

Jayson just rolled his eyes at that one.

"We leave at noon," Mrs. Lawton said. "Oh, and Jayson?"

"Yeah?"

"Whatever that loud noise was before, upstairs, before you came down for breakfast? Go clean it up, please."

When it was time, they drove to the City Centre mall in the middle of Moreland and she took him into a store and bought him a few pairs of khakis, some shirts, and some socks and underwear. Then they went into Rockport and she bought him a pair of shoes that felt like sneakers when he put them on.

When she'd paid for the shoes and they were outside, he asked, "Can we be done now?"

"C'mon," she said, "that wasn't really torture for you, was it?"

"I felt like a tool."

"Because you were trying on new clothes?"

"I felt like I was dressing up for Halloween," he said.

"One more stop," she said.

"I don't *need* anything else. What I need is to go *home*."

"That's exactly what I had in mind," Mrs. Lawton said. "We're going to the Pines so you can pick up your things."

When they arrived at the Pines, he told her he wanted to make it quick, didn't want to talk to anybody. He just wanted to pack his old life into the big duffel bag Mrs. Lawton had brought with them. One duffel and one box. Jayson had asked for the box to carry his trophies.

As they left the apartment, Mrs. Lawton stopped and looked around. "I remember growing up in the area, playing with my friends by the railroad tracks. I loved my friends . . . but I couldn't wait to get out of this town. I was going to leave and never come back."

Jayson stopped and looked at her. "You too?" he said.

She laughed. "What, you think I liked being poor? My dad was a drunk and my mom had left us. Daddy tried, but he never knew how to see beyond his next drink. The trick was convincing myself that I could do better. Education was going to be my way out."

"Basketball's mine," Jayson said. "What made you come back to Moreland?"

Mrs. Lawton smiled. "Home is a funny thing," she said. "You never know how important it is until you leave it."

They drove back to West Moreland in silence.

Up in Jayson's new bedroom, Mrs. Lawton placed the clothing bags on the bed. Jayson put the box with his basketball trophies on the floor and kneeled down next to them. Back in the tiny apartment, he had wrapped each trophy carefully in T-shirts, sweatpants, whatever he could find to protect them.

As he began to unwrap them, Mrs. Lawton joined him on

the floor. Jayson felt something inside him close up.

"What are you doing?" he asked.

"Helping," said Mrs. Lawton, reaching for a trophy.

"I don't need your help."

"Show me one," she said. "What's that one for?"

As she reached out toward one of the T-shirt-wrapped trophies, Jayson snapped.

"I said I got this!" His eyes challenged her. "When I need your help, I'll ask for it," he said. "Would that be okay with you?"

"Jayson, I—"

"I earned them. Okay? Can you just back off?" Felt his eyes stinging.

"Okay," she said. He could hear the hurt in her voice. Jayson wondered if she would get angry at him. Waited for it. Instead, Carol Lawton simply stood up and walked out of the room, shutting the door behind her.

Jayson left the trophies in one of the drawers in his bedroom, keeping them safe—and out of sight—like always.

After a while, Jayson walked downstairs. There, on the kitchen table, was the box with the sneakers he'd tried to steal inside.

"I went back and made this right with the store," Mr. Lawton said. "I'm not saying what you did was right, we both know it was wrong. But if you needed new sneakers badly enough to do what you did, well, that says to me that you need new sneakers."

"Nobody asked you to do this," Jayson said.

"You're right, nobody did," Mr. Lawton said. "But you told Kate Moretti that you stole these because you'd grown out of the ones you had and had no way to replace them. She told me how important basketball is to you. If you're going to play, you need shoes."

Jayson was still staring at the box, like somehow it had followed him all the way here.

"I can't take them," he said.

Mr. Lawton said, "You can't take them, or you don't want them anymore?"

"Both."

"May I ask why?"

"Does it matter? Just take them back."

About an hour before dinner, Jayson put on a baggy pair of North Carolina shorts he'd found at the Goodwill store and one of Tyrese's old Hornets T-shirts.

He stuffed his feet into his old sneakers, wanting those sneakers in the box but not allowing himself to show it. Then he went downstairs. He'd seen a hoop from his bedroom window, with a nice-looking half-court in front of it, a lane painted on it, a free-throw line, a three-point circle around the outside.

Mr. Lawton was still in the kitchen, the sneaker box still on the table. Mrs. Lawton was chopping vegetables at the counter, by the sink.

"Why'd you build a court like that?" Jayson asked.

"It was for our son," Mr. Lawton said.

"Isaiah," Mrs. Lawton added. "He thought that if he spent enough time out there, he'd end up at Cameron Indoor or the Dean Dome. But that's not the way it works, even if you grow up in Carolina loving basketball the way he did. And does. But now, he's going to be a great doctor someday."

Mr. Lawton smiled at that.

"So he's in medical school now? Isaiah?"

"Actually, Isaiah is taking a little break from school right now."

Jayson noticed that Mrs. Lawton had stopped chopping vegetables and was just staring at the cutting board. There was an uncomfortable feeling in the room now. Jayson wondered what was going on between the Lawtons and their son, but he wanted no part of it.

"So, the court," he said. "Can I use it?"

"This is your home now," Mr. Lawton said. "We hope you use it whenever you'd like."

Jayson mumbled a thank-you, but didn't move. Mr. Lawton raised his eyebrows at him.

"Is there a ball?" Jayson said.

"Ah, yes. The ball. You'll find a couple in the garage."

Jayson found a couple of balls on a shelf in the garage, along with some dusty basketball trophies. He picked up the more beat-up of the Spaldings, bounced it to make sure it wasn't short on air, and headed to the court.

He walked across the lawn, spinning the ball on the index finger of his right hand, almost like it was second nature to him. When he got to the court, he saw that it was sweet, even better than it had looked from the house. No little potholes in it, no raised cracks of asphalt like you got all over the court at the Jeff.

Mr. Lawton had said it was his court now. Like he owned it or something. Fine with him. When he was by himself on the court at the Jeff, he was always worried somebody would show up and interrupt his practice or his drills, interrupt him working on his *stuff.*

Just one more way he was always looking over his shoulder.

Not here, though, not now, on this perfect little court in the big backyard, perfect green grass all around it, the only sound the bounce of the ball. Or the swish of hitting nothing but net.

A couple of times Jayson looked up at the house and caught Mrs. Lawton watching him from the kitchen window. But he didn't wave, or even acknowledge her.

Instead he just turned and went back to playing ball, dribbling with both hands, going between his legs and behind his back, driving to the hoop from both sides, shooting from beyond the three-point arc, practicing shots in the lane, where he'd see how long he could hang in there before making a teardrop off the backboard or a floater.

He allowed himself to get lost in ball now, felt happy for the first time since he'd felt that man's hand on his shoulder.

Told himself that as long as he had a ball in his hands and a court to play on, he would always be happy, could stop feeling angry at the world for a little while.

Even here.

JAYSON FELT LIKE A COMPLETE idiot.

He knew he *looked* like an idiot, in his ironed khakis and polo shirt with the little animal stitched on the front. And the brown shoes in place of his kicks.

Jayson had always hated the first day of school—part of it having to do with clothes, because most of the other kids usually showed up in new ones. But there was something else that he hated about the first day of school: pretending to act happy to be back, like he was boys with guys he didn't even like that much. And he hated everybody talking about what they'd done during the summer, the places they'd been, even if they were from east side families without much money. At least they'd done *something* with their families.

Jayson? He'd been at the Jeff, like always.

Summer to him just meant more ball. In the summer, he never had to take a break from ball. He could play all day and into the night. He'd just keep on playing one game after the next, no matter whom he was playing against, no matter who was running the court. If there was no game, he'd practice, just waiting for the next game to break out. Usually the only time he left the court at the Jeff was to play in a summer-ball league somebody had started at the East Side Y for kids who weren't traveling with AAU ball.

In his mind, all school had ever been was time away from the court.

Now, taking the short ride to Belmont Country Day with Mrs. Lawton, it was like he was starting the school year all over again. She'd told him they had to get there early so he could meet the headmaster, the Lawtons having set up the meeting the day before.

So they met the headmaster, Mr. Rubin, and then he introduced Jayson and Mrs. Lawton to the head of the middle school, whose name Jayson forgot as soon as he heard it. The head of the middle school was the one who gave them a quick tour of the building and then showed Jayson where his locker was located.

Jayson kept thinking that usually, at this time of the morning, he'd be waking up at the Pines, wondering if there was still enough milk for his cereal. Or if he had any cereal left.

He'd brought his basketball stuff—and his old sneakers—with him in the new gym bag Mrs. Lawton had bought for him when they'd gone shopping. He knew he'd be meeting his coach and his teammates at practice. On Sunday, Mr. Lawton had gotten the names of the other kids on the team from the school. Jayson thought he recognized some of the names from rec ball.

All day Sunday, and even on the ride to school, it had

begun to set in, *hard,* that a new life also meant a new team. He'd been picturing all the guys at Belmont Country Day wearing their own khakis even on the basketball court. He'd already started thinking of it as Belmont Khaki Day.

But he would worry about that later. For now his thing was getting through the school day, going to smaller classes than he was used to at Moreland East Middle, maybe a dozen kids to a class, some of the same kids moving with him from math to English to history.

The teachers all made him stand and introduce himself to the class, making him feel like some sort of trained monkey. When it was time for lunch, he stopped at his locker and dropped off his history book. The kid next to him, a light-skinned black kid he recognized from English, said, "You know where you're going from here?"

Jayson shrugged.

The kid put out his fist. Jayson had no choice but to give the boy a fist bump.

"I'm Bryan Campbell," he said.

"Jayson Barnes."

"I know; I played against you in rec last year."

Jayson took a better look at Bryan now and thought he remembered playing against him once or twice.

"Oh yeah," Jayson said. "You were on the Spurs."

Bryan nodded. "Yeah, too bad we didn't make the playoffs."

Jayson wasn't surprised. The only one who could really ball on the team had been their center.

"I remember you had a big white kid who could really play," Jayson said.

"Cameron Speeth," Bryan said. "He goes here, too. You'll meet him later. Everyone on the team knew you were coming today."

"How'd they find out?"

"Facebook."

Jayson wondered if that meant people knew from Facebook that he was a thief who'd landed in foster care. But if Bryan Campbell knew, he wasn't saying anything about it.

Jayson moved the conversation back to the team. "I guess I gotta try out for the team or something after school."

"Nah," Bryan said. "Coach has seen you play."

Jayson was surprised to hear that. He knew he deserved to be on any team in the county, but it seemed pretty weak for a coach to just let a kid walk on without trying out.

"You'll meet Coach and the rest of the team at practice," Bryan said. "C'mon, let's go eat."

Jayson followed him down the hall, telling himself there were just three more hours or so until basketball.

He could smell the food as they approached the open cafeteria doors, and he said, "Guys on the team must be chafed, adding a guy after everybody's been picked."

Bryan stopped and gave him a look. "Did you want to win at your old school?"

"Of course."

"Well, we want to win just as bad. Before you got here

today, we figured that Moreland East Middle was the best team in the league—now we are."

Bryan laughed. "No pressure, though."

Bryan didn't ask Jayson if he wanted to have lunch with him, he just led him to the back of the line, handed him a tray, and told him how much he was going to love the food here.

"We even have pizza today," Bryan said. "Monday is pizza day."

They did have pizza. Hot pizza. Second time in a couple of days for Jayson. After months of being hungry, surviving mostly on peanut butter sandwiches, it felt weird to have hot food all the time.

"Let's go sit over by the window," Bryan said after they'd made their way through the line.

Jayson had piled his plate with food, but Bryan didn't make any comments about it.

Jayson followed him toward some empty seats at the end of a table mostly filled with girls.

"Do we gotta sit by the window?" Jayson said.

"What, you afraid of girls?"

Jayson felt the heat rising. "You joking?"

Bryan saw the look in Jayson's eyes and kept quiet.

Thing was, though, Jayson did get nervous around girls.

He didn't talk much to them, didn't understand them, never spent any time with them outside of school. Bottom line? He didn't understand girls any better than he understood how life had let him end up living with foster parents.

Put him on a court, even with bigger kids, and no worries, he was fine. That didn't scare him. He didn't scare very easily, not even when he'd been living alone, having to survive on his own. He hadn't even been scared when he had to steal—until he got caught.

Girls were a different story.

Jayson tried to fake his way through, though, put on his best fake smile as Bryan sat down at the table.

There were six girls at the table, three on either side, laughing and talking and sometimes holding up their phones so the others could see what was on them. The head of the middle school had told Jayson earlier that you were allowed to use cell phones in the cafeteria. Having never owned a phone, it didn't matter to him one way or another.

Everyone seemed to be talking about something they'd seen on YouTube or Instagram, or read on Twitter, almost like they were living in the virtual world instead of the real one.

Jayson wasn't surprised. He'd always noticed that kids who did have phones, especially the kids who couldn't go two minutes without checking them when they weren't in class—and maybe even then, on the sneak—acted as if the stuff happening to them in their lives didn't matter if they couldn't post it somewhere.

Jayson just put his head down and kept eating, half-listening as Bryan talked about the guys on the team and their coach. When Jayson finally came up for air, he saw one of the girls picking up her tray, and walking down to where he and Bryan were sitting. She sat in the seat next to Bryan.

"Mind if I join you?" she asked.

She was the prettiest girl Jayson had ever seen. He hadn't noticed her before, because a different girl had been blocking his view. But now here she was, right across from him. She had long blonde hair, blue eyes, and was wearing a shirt that seemed to be the same color as her eyes. She was smiling. Jayson couldn't explain it—he could barely think straight or breathe normally—but it was the best smile he had ever seen.

"Hi," she said. "I'm Zoe."

She waited for a response.

But Jayson didn't say anything.

"Zoe Montgomery," she said, louder this time.

"Zoe pretty much runs our school," Bryan said, as if he sensed that Jayson needed help here. "She just lets Mr. Rubin think he's in charge."

Zoe smiled at Bryan before turning back to Jayson. "You're Jayson, right? We were in English together."

Jayson managed a nod, then went back to eating what was left on his plate, which wasn't much by now.

"Does he speak?" Zoe said.

"A man of few words," Bryan said.

"Or no words," Zoe said, a big grin on her face.

She was still smiling when Jayson looked up again. It seemed this girl could carry on a conversation all by herself.

"I heard some of the other guys on the team talking about you in the common room," Zoe said. "Cameron told me it's going to be a whole lot more fun playing with you than against you."

Jayson had no idea what to say to her, so he kept drinking his iced tea, just to have something to do.

But Zoe Montgomery didn't give up. It was like she'd decided they were going to have a conversation whether Jayson wanted to or not.

"This must be so weird for you," she continued. "New school, new team, all new kids."

Jayson took one last look at her, helpless, not knowing how to talk to a girl like this, wondering how he'd ended up in this mess. Then he looked around the cafeteria, saw all the other boys wearing lame khakis just like the ones he wore, saw kids looking at their fancy phones, and he hated where he was in that moment.

He felt Zoe's eyes on him as he walked back across the cafeteria and out to the hallway.

9

WHEN SCHOOL LET OUT AT three, Jayson stayed in the common room waiting for basketball practice to start at four, his history book open in his hands. He wasn't really getting the jump on his homework, he just thought if he acted as if he were reading, people would leave him alone. Which they did.

When someone new would walk into the room, he'd look over his book, praying it wasn't Zoe Montgomery. Though maybe a small part of him hoped she would walk in, just so he could see that smile again.

When it was time, he headed down to the boys' locker room. Usually he couldn't wait to get on a court, any court, and start playing ball again. All day long he'd been telling himself to get through his classes because basketball was waiting for him at the end of it all.

But now that it was practice time, he just wanted to be on the other side of town, in the small gym at Moreland East Middle, with Tyrese, Shabazz, and the other guys from the Jeff. He hadn't spoken to any of his friends since he'd moved in with the Lawtons. He wondered now if they were missing him, or knew what had happened to him, especially since he hadn't shown up for school at Moreland East.

He knew Mrs. Lawton had called the school to tell them that he'd moved. Maybe by now his boys knew.

He pictured them getting ready for practice at his old school, pictured them happy, hanging with each other. There were parts of his old life that he would never miss. He'd never miss the ratty Pines, being hungry all the time, or having to steal. None of that.

But he missed his boys. Other than Tyrese and Shabazz, he'd never thought of the other guys as real friends. He'd told himself he didn't need friends to get by, or to get where he was going.

The boys' locker room at Belmont was at least twice the size of the one at Moreland East Middle. It was like a palace compared to what he was used to. The lockers were more spaced out and there were nice showers in the bathroom. It even *smelled* nicer.

Bryan showed Jayson where his locker was, then grabbed a red practice T-shirt that read "Belmont Bobcats" on the front, along with black shorts that had pockets, the kind that Jayson liked. Hanging in Jayson's locker was a white mesh pinny jersey for when they scrimmaged.

When he was changed and ready to play, Jayson said to Bryan, "How's your coach? Does he know what he's doing?"

They felt like the first words he'd spoken since he'd humiliated himself with Zoe at lunch.

"He's a great guy," Bryan said. "You're really gonna like him. He's one of the gym teachers here, and teaches English in the high school."

"But can he *coach*?" Jayson said.

"Guess you'll have to decide for yourself."

When they were on the court, before Coach Rooney showed up, Bryan introduced Jayson to the other players. It turned out he did recognize most of them from having played against them in rec leagues.

Cameron Speeth had grown since Jayson had last seen him, and grown his hair longer, too, but he was still as skinny as Jayson remembered. Phil Hecht was the team's starting small forward and Rashard Walsh was at power forward. Max Goldman was another small forward, sharing time with Phil Hecht. Alex Ahmad, the team's point guard, shook Jayson's hand.

Alex grinned and said, "I'm the point guard, at least for now."

Not for long, Jayson thought.

Bryan and Marty Samuels were both shooting guards. Marty Samuels was built more like a football player and looked like one, his blond hair shaved close to his head. He bumped fists with Jayson.

After Jayson met his new teammates, they all shot around

until they heard a voice say, "Two lines for layups." Jayson turned and saw a short guy who had to be Mr. Rooney, wearing a red Belmont T-shirt of his own, black sweatpants, a whistle around his neck, and old-school white Adidas sneakers with blue stripes.

He came walking over to Jayson. "I'm your new coach. Welcome to the team."

"Thanks."

"It's a good group; you'll like playing with them," Coach Rooney said. "Just make sure you work hard and put the team first."

"I always work hard," Jayson said, then added, "Coach."

He got into the layup line behind Cameron Speeth, his feet already starting to hurt from wearing old sneakers that were a size too small.

But he put the pain out of his mind, put everything out of his mind except basketball, telling himself that as much as he didn't want to be at this school, or playing with these guys, he was still playing the game he loved.

When they were done warming up, they went through some one-on-one defensive drills where you had to pick up a man at full court, press him hard, try to cut him off, do whatever you needed to do to keep him from getting past you without fouling him. Jayson was matched up against Alex Ahmad. Three times in a row, Jayson took the ball away from Alex before Alex came close to half-court.

When Alex was the one on defense, Jayson smoked him

with different moves, the last one a crossover that got Alex so jammed up he fell flat on his backside. Ball in his hands, Jayson flew down the court and drove to the basket—but instead of shooting a straight right-handed layup, he pulled the ball down, went underneath the basket, and made a reverse layup with his left hand.

He turned to look at Coach Rooney, thinking he might get some kind of reaction, thinking his new coach might tell him off for being too fancy. But all he got was a blank stare, before Coach turned and walked to the other end of the court.

Coach Rooney walked the team through some of their plays, mainly for Jayson's benefit. Most of them worked off a high pick-and-roll, guys spreading the floor, which was perfect for Jayson. That was his kind of game—pushing the ball down the court on a fast break, out-dribbling his opponent, finding the open man with a perfect pass. All he needed was some room to operate. Once you put the ball—and the game—in his hands, you could trust him to make the right decisions.

One of his old coaches had said, "The only thing you do better than create space, kid, is take advantage of it."

If only his new coach would know enough to give him his space, let him play his game.

"You need to pass the ball around more," Coach Rooney said to Jayson, telling him to hold the ball as he dribbled up toward half-court. "You know the way Tony Parker and the rest of the Spurs keep the ball moving? That's the way the game is meant to be played."

"There's just one way?" Jayson said, a note of defiance in his voice.

Coach Rooney held his look, long enough so that it was Jayson who finally looked away.

"I don't know how it worked at your old school," Coach said, "but in this gym, we do things my way."

The first team today was Alex, Marty, Max, Rashard, and Cameron. For the first time in his life, Jayson played with the second-stringers. Bryan was at shooting guard, Brandon Carr, who looked overweight but had good footwork and speed, was the backup center, and their forwards were two kids named Kyle and Brent.

"We'll play to ten points," Coach Rooney said. "Push it every chance you get. Man-to-man defense for now, we'll try out a 2–3 zone tomorrow. The losing team has to run gut busters."

Jayson knew about gut busters, but having won so often in scrimmages with his old team, he'd barely ever had to run them. When you ran a gut buster, you had to line up under a basket, then run to the free throw line and back. Then to half-court and back. Then to the other free throw line and back. Then up and down the length of the court. At the end of a practice, legs aching, lungs on fire, you'd rather be doing homework than running gut busters.

He didn't plan on running gut busters after his first practice or any practice. He was ready to play.

Jayson scored the first two baskets for the white team, beating Alex on one drive, then forcing Cameron into a switch on a pick-and-roll. He came hard at Cameron, like he was planning to drive past him, same as he'd done to Alex on the previous play. But then, at the last second, Jayson created space, backing up to get away from Cameron's long arms, and knocked down a jumper.

Brandon Carr had been open underneath, but Jayson ignored him. He wanted to show the guys on the team how good he really was.

As he was getting back on defense, he heard Coach Rooney say, "Layup there for BC if you'd wanted it."

"I didn't," Jayson said, mostly to himself, but not caring whether Coach heard him or not. He was playing mad like he always did, not letting anyone, even their coach, get in his way.

Halfway through the game, the score was tied at 5. Jayson knew he was just scrimmaging, but he was playing like it was the NCAA finals, defending Alex with a full-court press, forcing him to pass even though he was the red team's point guard, going out of his way to show Alex up and have someone else bring the ball up.

But Jayson had always played at full speed. It didn't matter if it was practice or the league championship, he'd never cared about hurting his opponents' feelings if they were trying to beat him. If you were on the other team, then you weren't his friend. Plain and simple. Tyrese liked to say that his boy Snap couldn't dial things down, because the boy didn't even *have* a dial.

The game tied at 7, Jayson ran down the middle of the court on a fast break with Brandon, exploding past defenders, showing his speed, Brandon on his left, forward Kyle on his right. Jayson got doubled at the free throw line by Kyle's man, which left Kyle wide open, running toward the hoop, but Jayson wasn't passing the ball to him. It hadn't taken Jayson long to figure out that Kyle couldn't catch a ball cleanly on the move to save his life.

Instead, he fired the ball up against the backboard, like he'd shot it way too hard. Only he wasn't shooting, he was passing, bouncing the ball perfectly off the board and into Brandon's hands.

Now Brandon got his open layup.

"Not exactly the bounce pass I was looking for," Coach Rooney said.

This time Jayson made sure everyone, including his coach, heard him loud and clear.

"Why does it matter, if the play worked?" he said.

Still no reaction from Coach, so he added, "Even if I wasn't doing things your way."

He was trying to push the guy's buttons, they both knew it. Every player on the court knew it. But still, his new coach showed no reaction.

The red team came back with a quick score of its own, Marty Samuels hitting a shot from the outside corner. On the next play, Jayson ran off a pick Brandon had set for him. Cameron switched again, and got those long arms of his up in the air. He put his hand right in front of Jayson's face, just like he'd been doing all game on the switch. Jayson cut left, and

Cameron's hand, which was all *up* in his grill now, brushed against the side of his head, a clear foul.

But coach didn't blow his whistle. So Jayson decided that if Cameron could get away with it, he would play just as aggressively.

Trying to get some extra room to shoot, he threw a quick elbow that hit Cameron square in the face.

Coach blew his whistle just as Jayson stepped back and shot a perfect teardrop over Cameron. *Swish.*

Cameron went down hard, looking like a football player who'd just been *laid* out.

"Offensive foul," Coach said. "Shot doesn't count."

"You kidding me!" Jayson's voice filled up the whole gym. "You call that on me, but nothing when he slaps my face?"

Cameron got to his feet and stared Jayson down. "Thought you were supposed to be good. Must not be if you throw cheap shots like that."

"You saying my game's cheap?" Jayson said, jumping to his feet, getting as close to Cameron as he possibly could. Now Jayson was the one in *his* face.

Bryan tried to pull Jayson away, but Jayson pushed him so hard that Bryan nearly lost his balance.

"Get off me!" Jayson said.

Coach Rooney had seen enough. He blew his whistle, three short blasts. "Back off, Jayson," he said firmly. "And if you ever do that again, I'll send you straight to the locker room."

Coach was the one with some snap to him now, not just in his voice, but in his whole manner.

Jayson was breathing hard. "I don't take cheap shots."

Cameron had walked away, but he said, "You threw an elbow and you know it. As cheap as it gets."

Before Jayson could do anything more than eyeball Cameron Speeth, Coach blew his whistle again. "Red ball. Inbound it from half-court."

When Jayson turned to head back down the court, he heard one of his teammates say, "What a jerk."

He couldn't tell if someone on the red team or on his own team had said it. Could've been anyone.

"C'mon, forget it," Bryan said. "Let's just win the game now."

Jayson didn't respond. Just gritted his teeth. Ready to play.

With a bruise starting to form on his lip, Cameron scored a quick layup when his team got the ball back, easily beating Brandon to the hoop. On the next play, Bryan answered right back with another layup and the score was tied at 9.

Alex Ahmad took the ball down the court, exposing the ball with his sloppy dribbling, leaving an opening for Jayson to swipe it right out of his hands, practically *giving* Jayson the ball. The white team called a time-out.

Before Bryan inbounded the ball to Jayson, Coach told them to just go down and run a play they called "Carolina." Brandon would start the play by setting a pick at the top of the key for Jayson. If the pick worked, and the defenders were forced to switch, with the smaller guy on defense, Alex, ending up on Brandon, then Brandon was supposed to cut to the basket for an easy bucket. Game over.

But this time, Alex went around the screen, and Cameron stayed on Brandon. So Jayson dribbled to his right, to the foul line extended. Kyle came up then and set another screen for him, which created an opening for Jayson to pull a crossover to his left hand and drive the ball to the basket.

As he was running in the lane, though, he saw Bryan cutting down the baseline, on his way to the opposite corner. The way the play was drawn up, Bryan became an option if he could get open. And Bryan *was* open now, ten feet from the basket, running right to left. Wide open. Marty Samuels, who was guarding Bryan, had turned his head so he could put his eyes on Jayson.

Jayson didn't hesitate, throwing the ball off his dribble with his right hand, a bullet pass, the hardest one he'd thrown all day.

Only, just like Marty, Bryan wasn't looking either, and the pass hit him in the side of his face. He went down as if he were the one being tackled now, knocked down by a blindside hit.

The ball ended up out of bounds. But no one else on the team was worried about the ball; they were worried about Bryan Campbell, sitting on the ground, head in his hands.

He didn't stay down long. Not even wanting any help, he popped up himself, the side of his face already swollen, and told Coach Rooney he wanted to stay in the game. Coach told him he should get some ice on his face, but Bryan said that could wait until after practice was over. Coach patted him on the shoulder, telling him to run to the other end of the court and get a stop.

As Bryan ran alongside Jayson, he said, “No worries, dude. I’m good.”

He put out his fist.

Jayson left it hanging in the air between them. “Next time, pay attention.”

THE RED TEAM SCORED THE last basket, Marty Samuels making a long jumper even though Bryan had a hand in his face.

The white team had to run the gut busters. Exhausted from practice, anger filling up his lungs, Jason still ran as hard as he could to blow off some steam, barely glancing around at the rest of the players from the losing white team running alongside him. He was still steamed about losing a game his team should've won.

The other kids hit the showers when practice was over. Jayson just threw his school clothes into his bag and got out of the locker room as quickly as he could. As unhappy as he was with the way the scrimmage had ended, he was just relieved that his first day at Belmont was finally over.

Only it wasn't over just yet.

Coach Rooney was waiting for him in the hall.

"Mind if I walk out with you?" he said to Jayson.

"Do I have a choice?"

"Nope."

They walked past the common room and the cafeteria, Jayson's long day stretching even longer.

"I talked to your coach at your old school," Coach Rooney said. "And I know some of the coaches from your rec leagues. I didn't ask them what kind of player you are; you're going to get the chance to show me that yourself. I asked them what kind of teammate you are. And they all said you were a great one. A team player who loves to run the fast break and find the open man. They said other kids don't like playing against you, but just about all of them love playing *with* you."

Jayson didn't say anything. He wasn't going to respond to another adult who thought he knew stuff about Jayson's life without *really* knowing him.

"Jayson, I'm not going to blow smoke at you; that's not me," Coach said. "I can't change your past, and I'm not going to try. As far as I'm concerned, you and I are starting with a clean slate. Okay?"

"Okay."

"But what is *not* okay," Coach Rooney said, "is the way you acted today."

Jayson didn't say anything, just bit his lip to fight back the anger taking hold of him, the anger he could never stop when someone challenged him. On anything.

"I want you on my team, make no mistake about that. And so do the kids back in that room, despite the way you treated them. But *if* you're going to play on this team, you need to respect your teammates and your coach."

"I played the way I play," Jayson said. "That's just who I am. Always playing at full speed."

"No," Coach Rooney said. "You played *mad.* But what you've got to get straight is that when you show up for practice tomorrow, you cannot take out your anger on your teammates or on me. That's not allowed in my gym."

"Or what?"

Coach Rooney tilted his head now, frowning, like Jayson had confused him.

"Really?" he said. "That's how you want to play this?"

"I don't know what you want me to say," Jayson said. "I didn't ask to have this conversation any more than I asked to be at this school."

"But you *are* here, that's the thing. And you're stuck with me as long as you're at this school, and on this team, which looks like it's going to have a shot to win big. So you need to decide if you'd rather stay mad and lose a spot on this team, or if you want to act like a team player."

"I play mad," Jayson said. "I've *always* played mad. Doesn't mean I'm not a team player."

"Well, I'm asking—no, telling—you to keep it under control," Coach Rooney said. "What you need to do, starting tomorrow, is make the best of this situation or risk losing your spot on this team."

Coach Rooney paused, looking right at Jayson. "Am I making myself clear?"

Jayson nodded.

"Have a good night," Coach said, and walked back down the hallway to the locker room.

Jayson watched him go, then turned and walked toward the front door.

Not just wanting to get away from Belmont Khaki Day—wanting to get away from his new life.

Mrs. Lawton handed him the cell phone from his bedroom when they got home.

"I noticed you didn't take this with you. It may not be the latest update, but it'll more than do. It has some bells and whistles, like they all do these days," Mrs. Lawton said. "You want me to show you how to work it?"

"I'll figure it out."

"You didn't say much on the way home about how your day went," Mrs. Lawton said.

"Great," Jayson said, not caring whether she picked up on the sarcasm in his voice or not.

He left her standing there, went upstairs, and showered so quickly it was like somebody was timing him. He changed into a T-shirt and the worn-out jeans he'd brought with him from the Pines, sat down at the desk in his room, and fired up his laptop, a really old model handed down to him from his mom. He searched for Tyrese's phone number in the small list he had in his contacts.

He punched out the number on his new cell phone, the first cell phone call he'd ever made.

Went straight to voice mail: *"This is Tyrese. Leave a message and I'll hit you back."*

He left his number and told Tyrese to call him as soon as he could because they needed to talk.

He went down to dinner, but he didn't say very much while eating. Mr. and Mrs. Lawton tried to ask him about his first day at Belmont, like they wanted him to take them through it minute by minute.

Finally they gave up on asking about school, and focused on basketball practice instead.

"How's the team look?" Mr. Lawton said.

"Okay, I guess."

"Just okay?"

"We scrimmaged. I learned a couple of plays. Met the guys and the coach." Jayson wasn't about to tell them about his blowup.

"Wade Rooney," Mr. Lawton said. "I hear good things about him."

Jayson shrugged.

Then he said: "May I be excused?"

"You don't even know what we've got for dessert," Mrs. Lawton said.

"I'm kind of full."

"Do you have much homework?" she asked.

"A little. I got some done between school and practice."

"Well, have at it," Mr. Lawton said. "Duke is playing

Michigan State in that Coaches vs. Cancer tournament on ESPN later. Maybe we can catch some of it before you go to bed?"

"Maybe," Jayson said.

As he stood up, Mrs. Lawton said, "Jayson?"

"What?"

"I just want you to know that we're going to do this at your pace."

"Do what?"

"All of this," she said. "Getting to know each other. There's no pressure. Okay?"

Jayson nearly laughed. "No pressure, huh?"

Mrs. Lawton looked him in the eyes. "If there's anything you need, or anything you're not getting from Tom or me, or anything we're doing that's making this harder for you, I want you to let us know. We want you to feel at home here, Jayson."

He excused himself from dinner, just wanting to go to his room after a day of being hounded by his coach, his teammates, and now the Lawtons. When he was almost out of the dining room, he turned back around. "There is one thing."

"Yes?" Mrs. Lawton almost sounded excited.

"Please stop trying to act like you're my new parents and everything's okay," he said. "Because everything is *not* okay."

Jayson turned around and walked up the stairs to his room.

He took out his cell phone. This time, Tyrese answered his call.

MRS. LAWTON WAS BANGING ON the door. For the first time since he'd met the Lawtons, it sounded as though one of them was getting angry. Something about that felt good to Jayson.

"Jayson," Mrs. Lawton said. "If you don't open the door right now, I'll be forced to call someone who can. Easier to just open it yourself."

Tyrese spoke in a scared whisper. "At least talk to her."

Jayson was looking at Tyrese, but he spoke to Mrs. Lawton. "I've got nothing to say to you!"

"I get it, Jayson," she said from behind the door. "I get it. You don't want to talk, you don't want to be in foster care, you don't want to be at your new school. But *this* isn't solving anything."

Jayson just stared at the locked door.

"What's happening here," Mrs. Lawton said, "is a normal reaction."

There it was again. Another adult who thought she knew all about him.

"Open it, Jayson. Now."

"Dawg," Tyrese said, "you got to give it up now."

Jayson stood there for a moment, wanting to be anywhere else in the world, far away from the Lawtons. But he had played in enough games to know when he was beat. He sighed, got up, walked over to the door, and let Mrs. Lawton into his apartment at the Pines.

"How'd you find me so fast?" Tyrese had left as soon as Mrs. Lawton came inside. It was just the two of them now.

It made her smile. "Kid, you've got a lot to learn about cell phones."

"Meaning what?"

"The funny thing about GPS," she said, "is that you can use it to find directions, or it can be used to find *you*."

Mrs. Lawton stood up and told Jayson to carry the bike belonging to Isaiah Lawton down the stairs, and strap it to the bike rack on top of her car.

"Lucky I don't strap you up there along with it," she said.

Earlier that night, he'd waited until Mr. and Mrs. Lawton were in the den watching television, then quietly made his way down the back stairs and took the bike he'd seen in the garage the other day. Then he'd walked the bike out through a side door of the garage and rode it into the night all the way across town, heading straight to the Pines, having told Tyrese to meet him there.

Tyrese had been waiting for him in front of the Pines. They decided that Jayson would sleep at Tyrese's tonight, just calling it a sleepover. Tomorrow he'd come up with a plan and make his next move. Take back control of his life.

But first he'd wanted to chill with Tyrese, just the two of them. Talk to someone who actually knew about where he came from.

"You know you're like my brother," Tyrese said when they were in the apartment. "But even if there was room for you to live with us, it's not like you could just go back to our school like nothing happened. Not like they wouldn't find you in a *snap.*" He smiled at his own joke.

"I wasn't asking you to do that," Jayson said. "I just need a night to figure things out. I can't stay there."

"Don't jump ugly with me," Tyrese said. "But it sounds to me like your setup there is pretty sweet."

"But I don't belong there! I should be with you, Shabazz, and the rest of the boys at Moreland East getting ready to win the county championship. I should be at the Jeff."

"But things have changed," Tyrese said in a soft voice. "You can't live your whole life on a basketball court. Maybe you just need to give it all a chance."

Now Jayson was sitting in the Lawtons' living room like it was his first night there all over again. Mr. and Mrs. Lawton were telling him that, as difficult as this was, for everybody, he couldn't just up and run away like that.

"You told me that already," Jayson said. "That this is *normal.*" He put air quotes around "normal."

"Yes I did," Mrs. Lawton said.

She was wearing jeans and a T-shirt tonight, hair pulled back into a ponytail, making her look more like some young girl than a woman trying to play the role of his new mom. She even wore some pink Nike Free sneakers. She was sitting next to a table that had a sculpture of a horse that she'd made resting on it. She'd told him once that she was an artist in her spare time; there were pieces of hers all around the house. But the horse, she said, was her favorite. Mr. Lawton said it was her best piece of work. Said that his wife had as much artistic ability in her as she had kindness.

"You scared us tonight, Jayson," Mrs. Lawton said. "We were so worried that something might happen to you while you were off on your own."

"Did fine on my own before you came into the picture."

"We care about you," Mr. Lawton said. "And we're trying our best to do right by you."

"I don't care!" he said. "Why can't you get that?"

"But *we* care, Jayson," Mrs. Lawton said. "We care that you give yourself the chance to be happy."

"The only time I'm happy in my whole life is when I'm playing ball."

Mr. Lawton said, "Your coach told us you didn't seem all that happy at practice today."

"You called him?"

"Yeah, I did. Carol called your teachers to find out how the day had gone. I called your coach."

"I'm not a five-year-old," Jayson said.

"Then maybe, and I'm just throwing this out there, you could think about not acting like one," Mrs. Lawton said.

She didn't say it in a mean way, and Jayson knew it. And she was smiling as she said the words.

"What do you want me to do, act happy so you can feel better about yourselves?" he said. "I'm not happy!"

"We know you're not," Mrs. Lawton said. "But you could be if you can find a way to give us a chance. And I have to tell you, because you need to know this, that if you run away again, Child Protective Services might be forced to relocate you. It would be out of our control—and yours. And that might mean you end up in a group home."

Jayson had heard horrible stories about group homes from other kids around the old neighborhood. From what he'd heard, they made the Pines sound like a luxury hotel.

Jayson felt tired all of a sudden. Boxed in. Trapped.

"I won't run again," he said.

"Good," Mrs. Lawton said. "Then that's settled. And from now on, Ms. Moretti has requested that you spend at least an hour a week together."

Jayson groaned. "More talking. Great."

"Remember what I told you," Mrs. Lawton said. "It's your

choice whether or not you make the most of this situation."

Same thing all the adults in his life had been telling him lately. That he had a *choice*.

"Whatever you say. Anything else?"

Mrs. Lawton shook her head.

Jayson went up to his room, stood at the window, and looked out at the Lawtons' basketball court, its lights turned off now. He sat back, lying in his new, comfortable bed, thinking about all those nights at the Pines, worrying about getting *the* knock on the door that would ruin his life. Thinking how, now that the knock had come, he'd gotten off pretty lucky, even if he didn't feel like he belonged here with the Lawtons. Then Jayson remembered the terrible stories he'd heard about group homes.

Thought about how he wouldn't let himself end up living in one.

The next morning Jayson took the new sneakers out of their box, put them in his gym bag, and left for school.

12

HE HADN'T BEEN LYING TO the Lawtons; he wasn't going to run again and end up in a group home.

It didn't mean he was going to trust them. It didn't mean he was going to let them in. He didn't have to let anybody in if he didn't want to, didn't have to let anybody get close to him.

Why would he? So they could die like his mother had? Or leave like Richie and every other guy had in the middle of the night?

He would focus on one thing, from now until the end of the basketball season: winning.

He was going to come out ahead in something. He was going to help the team from Belmont Khaki Day win the league championship and make it to the middle-grade tournament at Cameron Indoor. He wasn't going to let anybody or anything get in his way. But to do that, he knew he had to stop getting in his *own* way.

He'd made every team he'd ever played on in his life better. He was determined to make this team better, too.

Everyone kept saying he had a choice. But he didn't look at it that way—he had no choice but to make the best of things.

The next day at school, Jayson saw Bryan Campbell by his locker before lunch. Jayson could see that the side of Bryan's face was still swollen from where the ball had hit him.

"Sorry about yesterday," Jayson said. "Hope your face is okay." It sounded kind of lame, but it was the best he could do.

"All good," Bryan replied. "Really was my fault not keeping my head up to catch that pass."

Bryan closed his locker.

Jayson was about to leave for class when he called out to Bryan. "Can I ask you something?"

"Sure."

"Why are you still being nice to me? Especially after the way I acted at practice."

"You want the truth?"

"Always," Jayson said.

"Then I'm not gonna lie," Bryan said. "I've never met anybody who needed a friend more than you do. And if we're going to be on the same team, might as well have fun doing it."

Jayson felt blood rushing to his face. "I'm not looking for pity."

"Nah," Bryan said. "You're looking for a friend. You just don't know how bad."

Jayson wasn't so sure, but he knew that he at least needed his teammates in order to win games.

They ate lunch together. Without Zoe and her friends this time. But Marty Samuels joined them, and Brandon Carr, and even Cameron Speeth, whom Jayson nodded at—as good an apology as he knew how to give. Jayson felt that maybe Bryan had asked them to sit with him.

But somehow things were cool at the table. It's almost like they'd forgotten about what had happened at practice yesterday. Like they'd decided to move past it for the sake of the team. They all talked about the team, even Jayson joining in occasionally, because they all wanted to know what he thought about the other players. Cameron also asked about the team at Moreland East Middle and Jayson said, "We're loaded." Then he realized right away what he'd said, and changed it to, "*They're* loaded."

"Yeah," Marty Samuels said, grinning. "I hear they're weak at point guard all of a sudden."

"Not as bad as you think," Jayson said. "Tyrese can play point if he has to."

When the bell rang, they all said they'd see each other at practice, which wasn't starting until five o'clock today because Mr. Rooney had to pick up his wife at the airport.

It meant that when school let out, Jayson had an extra hour to kill. He knew he could have used his new phone to call Mrs. Lawton and ask her to pick him up and take him home for an hour or so, because of how close they lived to the school. He knew if he did, she'd drop what she was doing and come right over.

But he didn't want to ask her for a favor, because it would make him feel as if he had to do something nice for her in return. He was making amends with his teammates because he wanted to win, but he wasn't about to open up to the Lawtons. So he hung out by himself in the common room for a while and did most of his English homework. Then he went out and walked around the school campus, took a look at the grounds for the first time.

Football practice was still going on; the school team had one more game left in the season. And boys' and girls' soccer practices were about to end—a sport that Jayson had zero interest in when the World Cup wasn't going on.

When he got tired of walking around, he checked his phone, saw it was four thirty, and decided to circle back and start getting ready for practice, knowing that today had to be better than yesterday, that he couldn't do anything to *lose* basketball.

Bryan said he needed friends? He needed *basketball*, now more than ever.

He was thinking about that, thinking about making it to Cameron Indoor, what it would be like to play a big game there, when a ball hit him in the leg.

A soccer ball.

He looked down at the ball, then looked up and saw four girls in soccer uniforms and spikes walking straight toward him.

One of them was Zoe Montgomery.

Nowhere to run, nowhere to hide, no Bryan to do the talking for him.

He'd been wondering what was going to happen the next time he actually had to talk to her. He'd managed to avoid her in the two classes they had together—English and history—by getting out of both of them as fast as he could, with as quick a first step as he'd ever shown on or off the court.

Mostly he'd been wondering what he'd *say* to her, if he could manage to say something.

Now was his chance.

He reached down, picked up the ball, and tried to throw a perfect bounce pass in her direction. But you couldn't grip a soccer ball the way you could a basketball. He found out the hard way how slick it was.

The ball slipped out of his hand, badly, and went squirting off to his right. On *SportsCenter* one time, he'd seen a celebrity trying to throw out the first pitch at a Braves game. The guy was a lefty. But the ball ended up closer to first base than home plate, like he was trying to pick off an imaginary runner.

Zoe stopped. So did the girls with her, all of whom Jayson recognized from lunch the day before. The other girls laughed at his clumsiness, but Zoe didn't. She just stared at the ball rolling away from them across the grass, eyes wide.

She turned back to Jayson.

"And you're a basketball player?" she said, giving him that smile again. Jayson saw how great it was, even from a distance.

"It slipped," he said.

Then he jogged after the ball in his new sneakers; he'd been wearing them to break them in a little before practice.

Brought the ball back to her. Happy he'd been able to say something to her this time.

"These are my friends," she said. "Lizzie. Alex. Ella. Guys, this is Jayson. I've heard he's a really good basketball player. Apparently we'll have to take that on faith." That smile again, lighting up her face.

"I'm just not used to the ball," he said. "Not a soccer guy. But my friends who played, back at my other school, said I'd be good at it."

"Oh really?" Zoe said. "Because you're fast?"

"I'm just telling you what they said."

"Well, it takes more than being fast to be a good soccer player," Zoe said.

Ella, taller than the rest, said, "A *lot* more. You've got to have moves. And know what to do with the ball on offense and how to take it away on defense."

"Sounds like basketball," Jayson said.

"Just without using your hands," Ella said.

"I always thought that was kind of weird," he said, turning to look at Zoe. "A sport that doesn't let you use your hands."

Zoe raised an eyebrow. "You mean the way you just used your hands so brilliantly?"

"I told you, it slipped." He took the ball back from her. "Watch this."

He put the ball on the tip of his right index finger and tried to spin it the way he would a basketball.

Not even close.

The ball just fell off his finger and dropped to the ground like he'd blocked his own shot.

So much for showing off, Jayson thought.

Zoe turned to the other girls. "Maybe that's his hidden talent," she said. "He's got hands that act like feet!"

They all laughed again. As embarrassed as he was, Jayson almost laughed with them. But he stopped himself. Maybe it was pride. The guy who hated to lose more than anything was losing big-time with this girl.

Just like he had at lunch on the first day.

"Stupid ball, stupid sport," Jayson said.

"So now soccer's not just weird," she said. "It's stupid."

"I just like *real* sports," Jayson said. "You know, the kind where people actually score more than one or two times a game."

"You think you could score on me?" Zoe said, smiling again, but issuing a challenge, they both knew it. Doing it right in front of her friends.

"You can't play one-on-one in soccer," he said.

"Oh yes you can," she said. "Even a soccer hater like you must know about penalty kicks."

"I didn't say I was a soccer hater," he said.

"Saying soccer isn't a *real* sport pretty much means you don't respect the game. So why don't you teach us all how easy it is to score?"

He could feel his heart pounding now, being carried along

by this. Not just the challenge, but the fact that this was probably the longest conversation with a girl he'd ever had in his life.

"Okay," he said. "You win. I'll take you on sometime."

"Not *some*time. Right now."

"I gotta get to basketball practice."

"What time?"

"Five."

She reached into her pocket, whipped out her phone, and checked the time. "It's only four forty. Plenty of time for us to get this done."

"So it's on?"

"*Soooo* on," Zoe Montgomery said.

They walked back toward the main soccer field, the one Zoe said both the boys and girls used for games.

"Before we start we need to make a bet," Zoe said. "Just something to make things interesting. You're going to get a free shot at me in goal. You can put the ball on that line in front of the goal, ten yards away, like they do with a real penalty kick. Or if you want, you can do it like they do in hockey, and dribble in on me and try to beat me head on."

"How close can I get?"

"Close as you want."

"And what's the bet?"

"If you score, I show up for your first basketball game and wear a basketball jersey," she said. "But if you *don't* score on me, you have to come to my next soccer game and stand behind our bench wearing a soccer jersey."

"I think I'm getting set up," Jayson said. "Do I at least get to warm up?"

"As much as you need," Zoe said. "But remember, no hands this time."

She had some *snap* to her. He had to give her that.

Jayson and Zoe went out onto the field. All he kept thinking about was how he couldn't believe he'd let himself get sucked into this, but now that he had, he didn't want to embarrass himself, again, in front of Zoe.

He practiced dribbling the ball, making sure he could control it once he started running, not getting the ball too far in front of him, telling himself to pretend that he was just passing it to himself.

Then he went over near the goal, and practiced taking some shots, knowing he was going to go with his stronger leg, his right one, when it was time to shoot. He hadn't watched a whole lot of soccer, but he'd watched enough to know that they came at the ball the way placekickers did in football, from the side, planting their left foot—if they were kicking with their right—then swinging their leg through, sidewinder style.

He missed the goal with his first couple of kicks, but then started to get the hang of it, burying the next four in a row, two in the right corner, two in the left.

Like he was knocking down open jumpers.

"Good to go," he said to Zoe.

"You sure?"

"Let's do this," Jayson said.

"You want to place the ball on the line, or dribble toward the goal to shoot?"

If he wanted this to feel at least a little bit like basketball, he wanted to be moving.

"I want to dribble in."

"Go back as far as you want," Zoe said.

He moved back about thirty yards or so, to her right, planning to get to the middle of the field, about the place where you'd take a penalty shot, and then let the shot go.

His plan was to make her commit to defending one side first, and then he'd fire one into the part of the net she left open.

If he could outthink defenders on a basketball court, he could certainly do that with a soccer girl.

"Ready," she called out to him.

"Ready."

She put two fingers in her mouth and let out an amazing whistle.

Jayson started off slowly, pushing the ball ahead of him with his right foot, then his left, picking up speed, closing in on her, his eyes on that chalk line ten yards in front of her.

He could dribble a basketball without looking at it, and found himself able to do that now with this soccer ball. But as he got close to the line, he wasn't taking any chances, knowing exactly where he wanted to stop, knowing he needed to keep his eye on the ball when he was ready to plant and shoot.

That was why he never saw Zoe coming out of the goal like

a streak flashing by, kicking the ball away from him just as he was swinging his right leg.

Jayson kicked nothing but air, *both* of his legs flying like somebody had pulled a rug out from underneath him. He came down hard on the ground.

He turned and saw Zoe running—flying—toward the goal at the other end of the field.

"Hey!" he yelled after her. "You didn't say you could move!"

Without looking back, she yelled, "You never asked!"

She didn't even wait until she got close to the goal, didn't even appear to break stride as she fired a shot from what looked to Jayson like an incredibly long distance away from it, catching the ball cleanly, curving it into the net like a pro.

Only then did she make a slow turn to face him, hands on her hips, smiling wide at him like she'd just won the World Cup.

Jayson sat on the grass, watching her, feeling himself do something he hadn't done in a long time, certainly not since he'd moved to this side of Moreland.

Smiling.

THE THING ABOUT ZOE MONTGOMERY was, she just let him be.

She didn't seem all that bothered by his mood swings, and she made fun of him when she felt like it, without Jayson ever thinking she was actually trying to be mean. As far as he could tell after a week at Belmont, she didn't have any interest in changing him. It was a nice break from the adults in his life who kept telling him who he was and how he should act, what he needed, even how he should think.

Jayson didn't know how much she knew about his past, how he had ended up on this side of town living with the Lawtons, what his life was like before he got here. He figured she had to know at least *some* of it, but if she had questions, she hadn't asked them, at least not yet.

That was fine with him. He was just enjoying spending time with this girl.

Even with his limited knowledge of girls, and the limited amount of time he'd spent with them, Jayson could tell that Zoe was different. Of all the new people who'd become part of his life on this side of Moreland—the Lawtons, Ms. Moretti, the guys on the team, his teachers, and his coach—Zoe was the only one whom he really wanted to let in.

Somehow he trusted her, even though she'd never asked him to.

Ms. Moretti and the Lawtons were always talking about trust, how it worked both ways, *asking* him to trust them, to the point where he'd shut down as soon as he heard the word.

Zoe wasn't like that.

It didn't mean he felt comfortable being around her, or talking to her. But when he was with her, he felt like he could be himself. Whatever that meant.

He had said to himself that he wasn't going to be a phony, wasn't going to let his new life change him, but he knew he wasn't completely being himself at school now, or with the guys on the team, because he was making an effort to fit in. Trying to be one of the boys, making the best of the situation, thinking about a chance to play at Cameron Indoor if he could learn to accept his new team.

It wasn't as if he hated the guys on the team. They were actually all right. He was starting to work well with Cameron, their big guy, somebody Jayson knew would be able to hold his own, no problem, at the Jeff. Cameron could catch, shoot, rebound, defend. He wasn't afraid to play physical, box out hard, whatever it took to get a rebound or a stop.

The problem was that no matter how hard he tried, he just

couldn't think of the Belmont Bobcats as *his* team. He felt like he was some NBA player who got traded to a team he didn't want to play for.

It was weird, when he really thought about it. It took switching schools and switching teams to feel closer to Tyrese and Shabazz than he'd ever felt going to school with them. Hooping with them at the Jeff.

"You're still gonna chop it up when you start playing games," Tyrese said to him on the phone.

The season started in three days. Belmont's first game was against Karsten, and Moreland East was playing Moreland West in its opener.

"Of course," Tyrese added, "against us, you're gonna *get* chopped up."

"It shouldn't be this way," Jayson said. "I should be playing on *my* team."

"Things change," Tyrese said. "You got a new team now; start acting like it. And you know I'ma bring it when we play each other, so I expect nothing less from you, Snap."

"I never asked for any of this to happen."

"Yeah, but you were never one to cry about it or feel sorry for yourself. And even though you don't want to hear it, the way everything turned out, you're better off than you were living on your own at the Pines, having to steal peanut butter just to have something to eat."

"But if I was still there, I'd be playing with you guys. This all stinks!"

Jayson knew the Lawtons could probably hear him yelling from all the way downstairs. But as usual, his anger kept on boiling out.

"You got to chill," Tyrese said.

"Easy for you to say. You don't have to wear stupid khakis every day, pretending to be someone you're not."

"Go do what you do," Tyrese said. "Get a ball and take it out on the court."

He'd finished dinner with the Lawtons an hour ago. It had been another night when Mr. Lawton had asked Jayson to watch a basketball game with him, another night when Jayson had told him he had homework to do, even though he'd already finished it at school. Just another night when it felt as though Jayson was only visiting this house instead of living in it.

At least he was being himself.

He told Tyrese he'd talk to him tomorrow, put down the phone, and laced up his new sneakers. He'd broken them in nice by now. He slipped on some long gray sweatpants Mrs. Lawton had gotten him with "Belmont" written down the side, and an old Moreland East hoodie with a hole under the arm.

Wearing clothes from his old school and his new one. Like he was partly there and partly here. Caught in the middle somewhere.

Before he headed downstairs to get a ball out of the garage, he went over to his dresser and picked up his biggest trophy, his rec league MVP trophy from the previous year. There was a basketball player dribbling a ball on top. But you could lift that part up, and the base of the trophy was empty inside.

Inside of it was the envelope that contained the photograph of him and his mother. It was the only picture he had of the two of them.

They were standing in front of the Six Flags outside of Percy. Jayson had been nine when the photo was taken. His mom had been going through what he always thought of as one of her "good" stretches, not looking as sad or skinny or wasted-away as she had looked just before she died.

She was smiling in the photograph, her arm around him, holding the stuffed animal dog he'd won for her sinking softballs into an old-fashioned milk barrel.

Jayson would take it out sometimes, like he was doing now, just to stare at it, wondering if that was the last time he'd really felt safe in his life.

Not the kind of feeling you got living in a nice house, in a nice neighborhood, with people like the Lawtons—people who he knew, in his heart, were nice. Not that. But the kind of safe where you felt like you were where you were supposed to be. And that the person you were with was the one you were supposed to be with.

He had nobody like that now.

The only place where he felt that way now was on the basketball court, with a ball in his hands.

He didn't tell the Lawtons he was going out to shoot around. They'd figure it out as soon as they saw the lights go on. At least they didn't freak out anymore when they called to him upstairs and he didn't answer right away, just because he was listening to music, or taking a shower, or talking to Tyrese on the phone. He'd promised them he wouldn't run, and a promise was a promise.

Thinking about how quickly his life had changed, how easily it had been taken out of his control, his old team—and life—a thing of the past, he played like he was putting himself through a different set of gut busters. Driving in for a layup, driving the ball back outside, again and again, right hand, left hand. Dribbling hard toward the basket, pulling up and shooting a J or a teardrop, getting that feeling you got in a game when your legs started getting tired but you still had to use them to elevate.

Then he played Around the World. Layup, corner shot, foul line extended, foul line, until he worked his way back to another layup to complete the circle, seven shots in all. If he missed, even the last corner shot before the last layup, he'd go back to the beginning and start all over again. Pushing himself now.

He knew it was the way he was wired on a basketball court, constantly trying to improve his game, no matter how hard he had to push. This was the only way for him to work out, and try to let out as much of what he knew he was carrying around inside of him as he could. Work out his anger and his game at the same time.

Jayson didn't know how long he stayed out on the court. But he was dripping with sweat by the time he finished, even in the cool night air. Not so much tired from playing basketball as he was from thinking about going back to Belmont

Khaki Day tomorrow and going through the motions of trying to fit in, trying to belong or at least act like he belonged. Doing all he could to hide his old life from the people in his new life. Terrified that his teammates, or even worse, Zoe, would find out he'd been a thief.

This was another time when he was wondering what the look on her face would be if she ever saw the Pines. Wondering if it would change how she acted toward him, or thought about him.

Maybe she thought she was seeing him as he really was. And maybe he was closer to being himself with her than anybody else.

But the truth was, she had no clue.

He pounded the ball hard on the stone walkway leading back to the house from the court, went through the garage, shut off the court lights, still enjoying the feel of the ball in his hands as he came into the house. He was still breathing hard. Still felt the game running through his veins.

He heard Mrs. Lawton call to him from the living room before he could safely make it up the stairs to his room. Sometimes Jayson thought the quickest first step he had was on his way to that room, seeing how fast he could get up those stairs and shut the door to get away from the Lawtons.

"Jayson? Could you come in here for a second?"

He was caught, no way to avoid her. He walked through the kitchen and into the living room, ball on his hip. The Lawtons had paused the show they were watching on TV.

"What's up?"

"How'd it go out there?" Mr. Lawton said. "Working on your game?"

To Mr. Lawton's credit, he'd never tried to force Jayson to let him join him on the basketball court. Maybe he was smart enough to know that Jayson wanted to be alone when he went out there. So Mr. Lawton had never come out and tried to be a part of it, never tried to play the part of Basketball Dad. Jayson had to give him that.

"I'm always working on my game. It's how I get better." He paused for a minute, waiting for them to speak. "Is that what you guys wanted to talk about?"

Mrs. Lawton had a book on her lap. Maybe she'd been reading while her husband watched television. She took off her big reading glasses, the ones she'd wear in her small studio in the basement when she was working on one of her sculptures or when she was reading.

"No," she said. "I just wanted to ask you something."

He couldn't help himself, and sighed loudly—it just came out of him. He couldn't shake her, though. The sound just got a small laugh out of her.

"Is it that painful?" she said. "The question I haven't even asked yet?"

"Didn't say it was."

"Didn't have to."

He waited.

"It's just that I never hear you talking about the other kids at school," she said. "And we were just wondering if you've made any new friends, either on the team or from class?"

He had to end this as soon as possible. He wanted no part of any mother-son talk with Mrs. Lawton. "Nobody in particular. It's only been, what, like a week?"

He pictured himself making a smooth pivot, putting the ball on the floor, fast-breaking out the door . . .

"The reason I ask," she said, "is that I was talking to Pam Montgomery today. Zoe's mom. And she said that she got the idea that you and Zoe *had* become friends."

Just like that, the way it happened sometimes on the playground or in a game, with a shove or a comment or even a look, he felt the heat on the back of his neck.

"You were talking to Zoe's mom? About *me*?"

Even the words came out hot.

"What did you say?" he said.

"We just ran into each other at the grocery store and were having a conversation, is all."

"What'd you talk about?" Jayson asked, his anger so hot he felt like it would burn right through him. "Did you tell her all about how you had to take in a boy from the bad side of town? Did you tell her it was because I stole some stupid sneakers, that's why you had to take in poor Jayson Barnes?"

He was breathing even harder now than he had out on the court, wondering if Zoe finally knew all about him. About the sneakers, about the Pines, about his mom.

Like he'd been caught all over again. He felt humiliated.

"It wasn't like that, Jayson," she said, trying to keep her own voice steady, like she could calm him down with her words alone.

"Don't talk about me with other people!"

"Jayson, you're completely misunderstanding me. All I was getting at was that if you ever want to invite Zoe over, I don't want you to hesitate."

"Yeah, right. That's all you were getting at." He closed his eyes and shook his head from side to side, imagining Zoe's mom having a very different conversation with her daughter about him. Pictured the look on Zoe's face.

That's when he took the basketball off his hip and pounded it on the bare floor in front of him, the sound so loud it was like a firecracker exploding.

He wasn't prepared for how fast the ball shot back up, and as he tried to reach for it, all he succeeded in doing was pushing it in front of him like he was pushing it up the court.

After that all he could do was watch, helpless, as the ball bounced across the room in Mrs. Lawton's direction—nothing he could do to stop it as it hit the beautiful horse she'd made, like he'd been aiming for it, knocking it off the table.

They all watched as it shattered into tiny pieces on the living room floor.

JAYSON FELT AS THOUGH THE room was shaking. He hadn't wanted to break the horse, he just hadn't expected to lose control of the ball. He never lost control of a basketball.

But he was still so angry that Mrs. Lawton had gone behind his back and talked to Zoe's mother, told her who knows what about his life back at the Pines, that he wasn't about to apologize for breaking the horse.

Now's the time to tell me, Jayson thought. *Tell me I'm not good enough to be here.* But Mr. and Mrs. Lawton clearly knew that what happened was an accident. He could see them struggling, but they both stayed calm. It only made Jayson feel worse.

He slammed his hand against the wall and turned his back on the mess on the floor.

"Jayson," Mr. Lawton said.

Jayson glanced over his shoulder. He stood still, waiting.

Mr. Lawton continued. "Perhaps it would be best if you went to your room for now."

Mrs. Lawton had gotten down on her hands and knees and

was picking up the broken pieces, staring at them as though remembering having made each one. Mr. Lawton brought a garbage bag from the kitchen and held it open for her, his expression more sad than angry.

The ball was over at the foot of one of their bookcases. Jayson wanted to go get it. Wanted to turn back time and undo what had happened. Since he couldn't do that, he just went up to his room.

Later on in the night, Jayson sat on his bed, checking his phone for NBA scores just to have something to do, looking at some of the box scores, anything to take his mind off of the broken horse.

Despite all that had happened, Mrs. Lawton came in to say good night.

He put down the phone.

Jayson looked Carol Lawton in the eyes. He'd had some time to think about what had happened, leaving him with a sick feeling. "I just want you to know that I know how I'd feel if you came in here and broke one of my trophies," he said. "That horse was like a trophy to you, wasn't it?"

"I guess it was," she said. "But I can make another."

"You don't have to be nice about it."

"I'm not trying to be nice," she said. "I *can* make another. Somebody once told me not to miss anything that doesn't miss you." She sat on the end of his bed. "It was an accident, Jayson. Don't try to make it out to be something more than it was."

"I'm the accident."

"No, you're not."

"Yes, I am," he said. "You've got about as much chance of fixing me as you do that horse."

"You're not broken," Mrs. Lawton said. "You just need a chance to be whole. To be happy. To have a family. We want to give you that chance, Jayson."

"I proved all over again tonight that I don't belong here."

"You're wrong about that, too."

Mrs. Lawton got up now, reached over, picked up his phone. "It's late now," she said. "You should try to get some sleep."

Maybe on another night he would have argued. Not tonight. He was too tired to start another fight.

She put the phone on his desk and turned off the light. "We're stuck with each other, Jayson. And I promise that I will give you your space. But if you ever do need me, I'll be down the hall."

She closed the door behind her. All he wanted was to go to sleep and let the night come to an end.

Only he didn't sleep, couldn't sleep, not for a long time. He kept picturing the horse in the air, right before it hit the floor, trying to understand how—after everything that had happened to him—it was somebody else's trophy that finally made him cry.

FIRST GAME OF THE SEASON, gym at Belmont Country Day, Saturday afternoon, the Bobcats against the Karsten Kings.

First time in Jayson's life that the opening game had felt like some sort of finish line he was about to cross, just because of everything he'd gone through to get to it. Coach had told him that he was proud of the way Jayson had made a big effort at practice to get along with his teammates and be part of the team. Told Jayson he'd earned his starting point guard role.

Ten minutes before the game, Jayson went over to the home bench to take a swig out of his Gatorade bottle. It gave him a chance to look around. The Lawtons were in their seats up in the parents' section and, even though she'd won the bet, Zoe was sitting with her friends one section over. His teammates were shooting around, and then they formed two lines to take practice layups, wearing their white jerseys and shorts with red trim. The Karsten Kings wore Carolina-blue jerseys and white shorts of their own.

The only player that Jayson recognized from Karsten was

their point guard, Pokie Best, whose cousin lived at the Jeff, and who'd showed up a few times last summer to show off his game.

He nodded at Jayson when Karsten took the court, and Jayson nodded back. He figured Pokie remembered the two of them going up against each other at the Jeff as well as Jayson did.

As Jayson jogged back to the court, taking his place behind Bryan Campbell in the line, he saw Ms. Moretti making her way up through the stands to where the Lawtons were sitting.

As Jayson watched her take her seat, he thought about all the basketball games in his life when nobody had been in the stands to watch him play. But today he had three grownups watching him, plus Zoe, almost like he had his own cheering section.

He felt a hand on his shoulder and heard Brandon Carr say, "You just gonna keep staring up in the seats or you gonna keep the dang line moving?"

"Sorry," Jayson said. Then he broke for the basket, caught a pass from Cameron, took one dribble, released the ball, put it off the backboard in exactly the right spot, and didn't wait to see it hit the net. Just heard that sound as he walked away from the hoop.

He looked up at the clock. Five minutes to tip-off.

Coach Rooney went with the starting five they'd been using all week in practice: Jayson at point and Marty Samuels at shooting guard in the backcourt, Cameron at center, Phil Hecht at small forward, and Rashard Walsh at power forward.

Coach gathered the team around him. "What we're gonna

do today is play *our* game. Man up on defense. Remember on offense that the ball always needs to move faster than anybody trying to guard it. Pass, pass, pass, and find the open man. We're gonna play team ball because we *are* a team. Five guys on the court, one ball, one goal: to be the best team we can be each and every game."

He put his right hand out, his way of telling them to bring it in. They reached in and put their hands on top of his.

"One more thing," Coach said. "Hustle every single play. Every stinking loose ball in this game is ours."

Karsten won the coin flip. Their ball to start the game. When Jayson went over to match up with Pokie, Pokie said, "Heard you were with these guys now."

He was the same size as Jayson, wore his hair in cornrows, and smiled a lot on the court, though Jayson thought it was just part of his act, like he was the only one having fun.

Jayson shrugged. "Things change."

Pokie smiled his smile. "Long way from the Jeff."

Jayson answered by putting out a fist so Pokie could pound it. "Have a good game."

"Always do," Pokie said.

Jayson never tried to force anything early. He'd always watched LeBron let the game come to him in the first quarter, when he was with the Heat and now that he was back with the Cavs. That was his plan today, in the first official game with his new team, wanting to look sharper than he had in his first practice in this gym.

So he didn't take his first shot—a driving layup past Pokie on a crossover dribble, Pokie nearly tripping over his own feet—until there was a minute left in the quarter, his basket making the score 8–8.

Instead of playing like a ball stopper, Jayson was doing what he did best: running the fast break, finding the open man for a score. He had fed Cameron twice for easy buckets.

Then, Jayson drove through the lane, drew traffic to himself, and dished it to Marty Samuels for a wide-open jumper on the wing. But Jayson also had two turnovers, trying to do too much in his debut for the Bobcats, first forcing a pass to Cameron through a pack of Karsten defenders that was snatched up, then overthrowing the ball to Rashard by a mile when he tried to hit him with a long football pass on the break.

As soon as he'd seen the ball sail out of Rashard's reach and out of bounds, he'd looked over at Coach to see his reaction.

But all Coach Rooney said was, "Right idea. Less air under the ball next time."

Jayson had shaken his head, not at Coach, but at the pass, knowing Coach was right. Rashard had been wide open and he'd just missed him. Jayson was always focused on great passes, no matter where he was playing: the Jeff, Moreland East, or here with the Bobcats.

Anywhere there was a court, Jayson wanted to hit the open man.

He patted his chest, letting Marty and everybody else know

that it had been his fault. Not trying to let everybody else see how mad he was at himself, even after only one bad pass in the first quarter of the first game.

It had only taken him a few minutes to figure something out: You didn't have to love the school or even your new teammates to still hate making mistakes. Or love the game as much as you always had.

Coach Rooney sat him down at the start of the next quarter. Alex Ahmad went in for him at point guard, Bryan in at two guard, and Brandon Carr replaced Cameron at center.

"Sit next to me," Coach said to Jayson. "Let's watch the action together for a few minutes."

Coach Rooney didn't get up from the bench much, and he never yelled. When he did stand up, it was to say something positive, tell somebody they had made a good pass or stop or hustle play.

The rest of the time, he just talked to Jayson in a quiet voice about the game being played in front of them, seeing plays as they were developing, the way Jayson did sometimes on the court, thinking a move or two ahead, leaving his opponents a step behind.

Meanwhile, Pokie was *schooling* Alex Ahmad. Making it look like he was filming one of those AND1 mixtapes where the guys did trick plays, out-dribbling, out-shooting, and out-defending Alex. Pokie shot a J right in Alex's face, Alex barely getting a hand up, and the Kings were suddenly up eight points.

"Relax," Coach said to him at one point. "We'll be fine."

"I didn't say anything," Jayson said.

"You didn't have to."

"Were you a point guard when you played?"

"You can tell, huh?"

"You watch the game like you're playing it."

"Old habits die hard," Coach said.

Jayson sat longer than he wanted to, or thought he should have. By the time he got back in the game, the Karsten lead was twelve points, mostly because Pokie had been torching Alex Ahmad the way he had.

Then, when Coach moved Bryan over to defend Pokie, the Kings' point guard torched him, too.

Maybe that's why Jayson started forcing things when he stepped back onto the court, wanting to make things happen right away, overworking himself to make sure that Karsten's lead wasn't twenty points by halftime, and the first game of the season didn't turn into a blowout.

Karsten was ahead 28–14 when Pokie read a crosscourt pass Jayson tried to throw to Marty Samuels all the way, caught it as if Jayson were trying to send it his way, and took off for what looked like an easy breakaway layup.

Only, as fast as Pokie Best was, Jayson was faster. He didn't hang his head because of the turnover, or give up on the play. He could see that Pokie thought he was in the clear, didn't even think anybody was chasing him. But just as he pushed off for his layup, Jayson came around and blocked the shot cleanly out of bounds.

But Pokie went down as if Jayson had flagrant-fouled him, and the ref trailing the play blew his whistle. Fell for Pokie's blatant flop.

Jayson wheeled around, grabbed his head with both hands, and yelled, *"C'mon, ref!"*

The ref looked at him sternly. "You got him on the arm, son."

"I got all ball!"

"Not the way I saw it. Two shots."

"But you *didn't* see it," Jayson said. "You had a bad angle. All you saw was Pokie flopping."

He knew what Pokie was doing, begging for a call this way, especially after Jayson had chased him down and swatted the ball cleanly.

"You get fined in the pros for flopping like that," Jayson said.

Behind him, he heard Coach Rooney say, "Drop it, Jayson."

But Jayson wasn't dropping it; he was way too far into the moment now to turn back.

He said to the ref, "Next time try hustling back on the play like I did, so you can see what really happened."

That was it. The ref glared at Jayson, blew his whistle, gave the classic signal for a technical foul, palm on top of his fingers. Bang. Then he looked past Jayson and said to Coach Rooney, "One more word and he's out of the game."

Jayson felt Coach's hand on his shoulder then, spun around in anger, still hot, and said, "It wasn't a foul and you know it."

"It's a foul if he calls a foul," Coach Rooney said. He looked at Jayson hard, like he had at that first practice after Jayson had elbowed Cameron.

Then Coach signaled to Alex Ahmad to check back into the game.

THIS TIME, JAYSON WENT TO the end of the bench, far away from Coach, and stayed there, not talking to anybody, not looking at Coach or up into the stands. He wondered what the Lawtons were thinking, watching him turn into a lit fuse here the same way he had when he'd broken Mrs. Lawton's horse.

At least the Bobcats made a run before the half, almost all of it Cameron Speeth's doing. Cameron refused to let the game get away from Belmont even with Jayson on the bench, playing great at both ends of the court, scoring and defending like a one-man team, cutting Karsten's lead to eight, 32–24.

Coach Rooney pulled Jayson aside before he went into the locker room with the rest of the Bobcats. "Just so you know, I think it was an awful call."

"Why didn't you tell the ref?"

"Because he wasn't going to change it, and it wasn't going to do any good," he said. "And by the way? The coach who yells at refs? I'm never gonna be that guy."

"All I was trying to tell him was what you just said to me."

"Next time, don't tell him anything."

Jayson started to say something, but Coach put a finger to his lips. "Listen to what I just said, Jayson. You're allowed to think it's a bad call, because nobody ever gets T'ed up for what they think. But I don't want you to say another word to a ref the rest of the season, other than 'Yes, sir' and 'No, sir.' Because if you do, I will sit you down for the rest of the game. Understood?"

He'd heard an announcer say one time on television that the way coaches controlled players the best was with playing time. Thinking about sitting another minute on that bench, he understood why.

Jayson nodded.

"Be smarter in the second half," Coach said.

Marty Samuels picked up his third foul halfway through the third quarter, and Coach subbed in Bryan to play with the first team.

And Bryan Campbell came out hot, hitting four straight shots from the outside, two of them threes. The Kings, on the other hand, were missing shot after shot, and by the time the quarter ended, the Bobcats had the lead for the first time all game, 39–38.

As they came to the bench when the quarter ended, Bryan got close to Jayson and grinned at him. "I had a feeling good things might happen when I started catching your passes."

But Jayson wasn't ready for a victory celebration. "Still a long way to go."

He was worried Coach might sit him at the start of the fourth quarter the way he had at the start of the second, give Alex Ahmad a little more burn. But Coach stayed with the five that had ended the quarter, Bryan still in there for Marty.

As they broke their huddle, Coach said to Jayson, "I believe we have identified the one player they've got who can beat us today."

Pokie.

"I could have told you that before we started warming up," Jayson said. "But don't worry, I'm not letting that flopper beat us."

"Let it go," Coach said.

"I'll let it go when we win."

Pokie tried to get in Jayson's head the rest of the way, talking into his ear even more than he had over the first three quarters. But Jayson ignored him. He kept his focus on the game, telling himself that he'd made his last dumb decision of the day, and his last turnover, too.

With four minutes to go, Pokie, who wasn't a great outside shooter, stepped back to make a couple of jumpers even with Jayson up on him, tying the game at 48. And maybe if this had been a playground game, Jayson would have gone down to the other end and tried to match, put a couple in Pokie's face, like they were playing a game of H-O-R-S-E.

But this wasn't the Jeff. This was a game he was trying to win, his first game for the Bobcats, and that meant doing what he was supposed to do, making the guys around him better. Defend, run the ball down the court on a fast break, do what he did best. He felt like everyone, especially his teammates, was watching him more closely now than ever, every move he made, to see if he could close the deal.

But he'd felt all eyes on him since he'd shown up at Belmont, like they were waiting for him to mess up.

Jayson wasn't about to do that. Not today. Just over two minutes to go, the game tied, the Kings' center shooting free throws, he allowed himself a quick look up into the stands to the spot where the Lawtons and Ms. Moretti were sitting.

Ms. Moretti saw him, smiled, and pumped her fist at him. He nodded.

Let's do this.

Jayson took an outlet pass from Rashard Walsh when the Kings' center missed his second free throw, pushed the ball on the break, eyeballed Bryan the whole time on the left wing before turning at the last second and hitting Cameron, in stride, with a perfect bounce pass.

Bobcats up by two.

But then on the next play Phil Hecht lost his man, a skinny blond kid, in a switch, and the kid hit the first three he'd made all day. Kings by one.

The game seemed to speed up. The Bobcats came right back, barely taking any time off the clock, and Cameron made a short jumper just inside the foul line. Bobcats back up by one.

That wasn't enough to get Phil's head back in the game,

though. Right after Cameron's jumper, Phil committed a dumb foul on his man. The Karsten forward made both free throws. Kings by a point.

Forty seconds left.

Jayson took his time at the other end of the court, Pokie hounding him, but Jayson did a great job protecting the ball. He finally got into the lane and fed Cameron like he'd been doing all game, left side of the hoop. But Cameron missed a baby hook for the first time all day. Then Pokie beat everybody to the rebound.

Thirty seconds left. The Kings' coach called time-out with a one-point lead. There was a thirty-five-second shot clock in their league, which meant that Karsten didn't have to shoot. They could let the time run out and win the game, if they didn't lose the ball or draw a foul.

In front of the Bobcats' bench, Coach said, "Play them straight up and try to get a steal. If they've still got possession with around fifteen seconds left, foul somebody, even if it's Pokie. Even if he makes both free throws, we've still got a chance to tie with a three."

The other players nodded. Jayson said, "We're gonna get the ball before we have to foul."

"And when we do get it, no time-outs," Coach said. "I'd always rather push it than give them a chance to set the defense. Agreed?"

He addressed all of them, but he was looking straight at Jayson, like he was talking only to him. Like it was just the two of them in that moment, speaking point guard to point guard.

"Agreed," Jayson said.

Jayson pulled Bryan aside. "If I do yell at you to double Pokie, don't wait and don't worry about leaving your guy; run at him like a crazy man."

Bryan Campbell said, "I can do that."

Even before they were out of the huddle, Jayson was thinking one move ahead.

The Kings inbounded the ball. Jayson didn't wait to pick Pokie up in the backcourt; he employed a full-court press, attacking him all the way up in the frontcourt. Feeling the pressure, Pokie passed the ball off to his shooting guard, and then got it back with twenty seconds left.

Jayson yelled, "Double!"

Bryan played it the way Jayson had told him to, running at Pokie Best like an outside linebacker blitzing a quarterback. As soon as he did, Pokie did exactly what Jayson had hoped he would do: took his eyes off Jayson just long enough to make it count.

Jayson moved even faster than a basketball could, like a blur streaking by, tipping the ball away from Pokie, knocking it to the side, picking it up on a left-hand dribble, turning the play around, turning defense into offense in a flash.

He could see Cameron Speeth running like a madman down the right side of the court, Rashard Walsh cutting behind him, like they were both ready, like they knew Jayson would make something happen.

Jayson wasn't going to make the same mistake Pokie had made on the flop play. He turned his head just slightly, saw Pokie chasing him, trying somehow to get back in the play. Get the ball back and keep the Kings in the game.

No chance.

Jayson angled to his right, cutting Pokie off, forcing him to put on the brakes or risk committing a foul and sending Jayson to the line to win the game, Jayson having made all four of his free throw attempts.

He checked the clock now. Ten seconds.

With Pokie behind him, he thought he could beat anybody the Kings had off the dribble, get himself a layup or at least an easy shot.

But this wasn't the day to try to make a hero shot. This was a game to win with a pass.

Bryan, also trailing the play, was wide open on his left, having beaten his own man to one of his favorite spots on the court. Rashard and Phil had spread out to the corners. Lots of options.

But not his best option.

As Jayson dribbled into the lane, Pokie still at his back, having cut him off on the right, Cameron's defender was forced to come over to double Jayson and block his path to the basket.

Jayson let the ball go. The motion looked like the kind of teardrop shot he'd made in the first half, which was another time the kid guarding Cameron had switched off to double Jayson.

Only it wasn't a shot. Cameron knew it, too. The Karsten center put a long arm in the air, thinking he could get a piece of the ball.

But the ball wasn't floating toward the rim—it was heading into Cameron Speeth's hands, a perfect lob pass. Cameron caught it in stride and laid the ball in two ticks before the horn sounded in the Belmont gym.

The Bobcats had won by a point.

Maybe nothing else in Jayson's life worked out the way he wanted it to. But basketball still did.

17

MS. MORETTI CAME TO THE house after practice on Monday.

Jayson had gone out of his way since the game to try to be nicer to the Lawtons—Mrs. Lawton especially. He still felt bad about breaking her sculpture. Plus, now that the season had started, he wanted as few distractions as possible. That meant not creating any for himself.

He was trying not to let anything get in the way of basketball. Because basketball, he kept telling himself, was the only part of his life he had full control over.

He and Ms. Moretti sat in the den, just the two of them, the Lawtons having gone out for a walk before dinner.

"So how's it going?" Ms. Moretti said.

She was still in her work clothes: a dark jacket that matched her pants, a white shirt underneath. Her hair was pulled back. She didn't have her notebook out tonight, like she did sometimes. When she started taking notes, it made Jayson feel like he was some kind of school project for her: Jayson 101.

"You know you start off asking me the same question every

time you come?" Jayson said.

"I haven't been here all that often," she said. "And I generally ask that because, and I know this is going to sound crazy to you, I want to know how you've been doing since the last time I saw you."

"You saw me Saturday."

"I did."

She waited.

"I'm fine," he said.

"Just fine?" she said. "Dude, you've got to feel better about things after the way you and the team played on Saturday. That was some game. I felt like I was watching Duke–Carolina there at the end."

"It was just the first game of the season."

She shook her head, a small smile on her face. "You *are* tough."

"You have to be tough in basketball," he said. "Toughest guys on the court are the last ones standing. Everyone wants to win out there."

"Not the way you do."

"Maybe I want it more because I need it more."

She stared at him, but didn't say anything right away. Sometimes it wasn't just that she was waiting, Jayson thought; it was like she was trying to wait him out. Looking for an opening, so she could ask him another question about himself that he didn't want to answer.

"I just don't want basketball to be your whole life," she said. "There's so much more to you than basketball."

"You're wrong," he said. "You say you're getting to know

me, and you don't know anything about me if you think that way."

"How so?"

"Basketball's all I got," he said. "And it's all I want." The words felt like lies as soon as they left his mouth.

"You've got teammates," she said. "You have to rely on them. Trust them. You did when you made that pass the other day."

"It's just another way of trusting basketball."

"What about friends?" she said. "You've talked about friends you played with at your old school. How about at Belmont?"

"I've got teammates now, not friends."

"They can't be both?" she said.

"It's just easier this way," he said.

"Why? What's the worst that could happen if you open yourself up a bit?"

"I don't know," he said. "Disappointment. Or I could mess up again, get caught, and sent someplace new."

"That's not going to happen. Besides, messing up brought you here," she said. "Not so terrible, right?"

"Riiiiight," he said, not even trying to hide the sarcasm.

Ms. Moretti stood up. "I'm not your opponent, Jayson."

"Didn't say you were."

"All of us might be able to help you learn how to be happy, if you'd let us."

"Like it's some kind of basketball move you can teach me?"

That got a smile out of her. "If that's what works for you."

Sometimes Jayson had no idea what worked for him other than a sweet pass. But he wasn't going to tell her that.

He *wasn't* going to show her his moves.

THE BOBCATS WON THEIR NEXT game, against St. Patrick's. Jayson didn't play at all in the fourth quarter, because the 'Cats were winning by twenty. They were 2–0, heading into their home game against Tyrese, Shabazz, and the rest of the guys from Moreland East in a week.

The St. Patrick's game had been at ten in the morning, so Jayson had plenty of time to head back to the soccer field at Belmont for Zoe's championship game against Weston in the afternoon.

Jayson had lost a bet, and he intended to make good on it.

Bryan Campbell's parents had driven them back to Belmont from the gym at St. Patrick's. "She won't even know whether you're there or not," Bryan said. "We could skip out and go to an early movie."

"She'd know," Jayson said.

"Well, I like Zoe, too," Bryan said. "But I'm not watching a whole girls' sports match. You're on your own."

Jayson just shrugged.

A promise was a promise. And to be honest, he was

actually looking forward to seeing Zoe do her thing. Everybody at school had told him she was a total star.

"Well, you go have your soccer fun," Bryan said. "I'm out of here."

Jayson was actually happy that he was leaving. If he hung around, he might find out that Zoe had invited Jayson over to her house after the game. He didn't want to have to listen to Bryan busting on him over that particular piece of information.

Jayson wasn't going straight from the game to Zoe's house, though. If Belmont won the championship, the girls on the team and their parents were going to a pizza party in town. Zoe had told Jayson he could join them, but he said he'd pass. Hanging with one girl was already enough pressure for Jayson, let alone a whole soccer team full of them. Instead, he'd asked Mrs. Lawton to drive him over to Zoe's after the pizza party—if her team won.

"Isn't that like planning the victory parade before you win the game?" he'd said to her on the phone the night before.

"I thought you were the one always talking about thinking one move ahead."

"It doesn't mean you should get ahead of yourself."

"If we lose, we call off the party, no biggie," she'd said, before adding, "But we're not losing."

He wasn't nearly as worried about her losing as he was about her hearing about his past, his life before he'd come to live with the Lawtons and gone to Belmont Country Day.

He kept coming back to the same thing: The better he got

to know Zoe, the better the chance she was going to find out who he really was.

Jayson sat by himself in the bleachers. He looked around at the other people there to watch the game. Lots of moms and dads, their phones or tablets always ready to snap a picture or record the action. There weren't many kids from school, he noticed. A group of girls he'd seen hanging around with Zoe who weren't on the team. Eric Kelly, who Jayson knew was the star of the boys' soccer team, was on the sideline, dribbling a soccer ball, practicing some moves against an imaginary goalkeeper. And one other boy, who seemed to be taking notes. Jayson figured he wrote for the school paper or something.

It turned out to be a great game. Even though there wasn't much scoring, the defenses outplaying the offenses, it was obvious that Zoe was the best player on the field.

Neither Zoe nor any of the other scorers on her team could put the ball in the net early on. But what he realized now after watching the game this closely was that soccer would be fast and fun to watch even without goals being scored. Zoe was a midfielder—a center middie, she said—and she wore number 10 because that was the star number for center middies in soccer. She was constantly on the attack, setting things up, kind of like Jayson did on the court for the Bobcats. Looking at things from the perspective of a point guard, he loved the way the girls moved the ball, passed it around, and spread the field.

But with five minutes left, it was the two goalkeepers who'd been the big stars in the championship game. Zoe had hit the crossbar once in the first half, a couple of minutes into the game. With about ten minutes left, she'd blasted a huge shot at the Weston keeper that had just missed the far post. The game stayed zero–zero.

Or nil–nil, as they called it in soccer.

Then there were three minutes left. Jayson knew, because Zoe had explained it to him the night before on the phone, that because it was a championship game, they'd play a ten-minute overtime if the game was still tied at the end of regulation. And if it was still tied after *that,* they'd go to one of those World Cup–style penalty-kick shootouts to decide who would win it all.

With just under three minutes left, Zoe made a great pass to her friend Lizzie, and Lizzie ended up with what looked like a mile of open net, but she slipped at the last minute and didn't get enough leg behind the kick. The Weston keeper dove, got a hand on the ball, and knocked it away.

Weston's girls tried to push the ball down the field, but then Zoe did what she'd been doing a lot of during this game: turned defense into offense in the middle of the field.

Turned the game into the "Zoe Show." Now she was the one pushing the ball, flying up the middle of the field.

They're giving her too much space, Jayson thought, knowing space mattered as much in soccer as it did in basketball.

One Weston backer, then another, came up on her, but Zoe dusted them both off, making it look as if the girls on defense had suddenly forgotten just how fast she really was. Dribbling it with her foot the way Jayson could dribble a basketball on the fast break.

Another backer came from her right and briefly got in front of her, but Zoe pushed the ball through the girl's legs, and kept on moving forward like nothing had gotten in her way.

Now it was just her and the goalkeeper. Jayson knew the girl had to make a decision on the fly herself: whether to come out the way Zoe had that day when Jayson was trying to score on her, or choose to sit back, like the last defender on a fast break, and wait for Zoe to make her move.

The girl decided to hang back, arms out to the side, knees bent, bouncing a little on her toes. A perfect defensive posture for any sport.

And Zoe did make the first move, pushing the ball to her right, side-stepping that direction, even though Jayson saw from where he was watching that the motion cut down her angle considerably, giving herself less net to shoot at.

The goalie moved with her, just slightly.

As soon as she did, Zoe was ready; she came almost to a dead stop, acting as if she had all day, even though she had to feel the Weston defense coming from behind her. She made this cool stutter-step move as the goalie dove to her left, defending a shot that seemed as though it was coming off Zoe's right foot.

Now Zoe was the one thinking one move ahead.

The ball was on her left foot instead, and now the net was wide open. She buried the ball in the corner of the goal. Game over.

One–nil, Belmont.

JAYSON KEPT HIS DISTANCE FROM Zoe after the trophy presentation. This was her moment.

She was the one who found him after all the pictures had been taken, asking him again to come with her to the pizza party.

"Pass," he said.

She grinned. "Suit yourself."

"Nice play at the end there," he said.

She did her little stutter step and said, "You like that move?"

"You have to teach it to me sometime."

She said she'd see him at her house around four thirty. Her older brother, a senior in high school, was going to be there, too. Her parents were going shopping at the mall after the party.

She ran off to be with her teammates, joining in on all the selfie fun going on at midfield.

Later on, Mrs. Lawton dropped him off at Zoe's house. It turned out to be just a couple of miles from where the Lawtons lived—it was still the way he thought about it; their house, not his—in what looked to be an even nicer neighborhood, with even larger houses. There was a security guard in a little house at the gate who had to buzz them in after Mrs. Lawton gave her name.

When they pulled into the driveway, Mrs. Lawton said, "This neighborhood makes me feel as if I'm still on the wrong side of the tracks."

"Tell me about it."

"Will you be staying for dinner?" she said.

He shrugged. "Zoe just said to come over and hang out."

"Do you want me to call her mom?"

"No!" he said, almost before the last word was out of her mouth.

"Sorry," Mrs. Lawton said.

Jayson didn't want to go anywhere near the conversation about Zoe's mom that had ended with Mrs. Lawton's horse in pieces. He still thought about that night often, and always with regret.

He got out of the car. "I'll call you, okay?"

She pulled out of the driveway and he watched her car disappear. He didn't see any other people outside on the street. Even so, as he walked to Zoe's front door, he felt like the whole neighborhood was watching him from inside their big houses, thinking the same thing that he was—that he didn't belong here.

Zoe's brother answered the door. As he did, Jayson could see Zoe running down a long stairway behind him, saying, "I *said* I've got it!"

"Chill," her brother said. He turned to look at Jayson. "Jayson, right? I'm Chris."

He was tall, with long brown hair. Zoe had said he was a shooting guard on the Belmont varsity team.

"Heard you can play a little," Chris said.

"I guess."

"I *guess*," Zoe said. "My brother was just on his way back to his room to play more video games."

Chris grinned. "Nah, I'm good. I could hang with you guys if you want."

"And I could read all your text messages to your girlfriend the next time you leave your phone lying around if you want," Zoe said.

Chris grinned again. "She's all yours, Jayson." He patted Zoe's head on his way toward the stairs. She wheeled around and tried to give him a soccer-style kick, but missed.

Zoe was wearing a T-shirt, jeans, and the kind of canvas sneakers that didn't have laces.

"Sorry about that, my brother can be a little overprotective sometimes," she said. "What do you want to do?"

"Whatever you want," he said.

They were standing in the front hall, as if neither one of them knew what to do now that Jayson was actually at Zoe's house.

Finally, Zoe said, "You want to shoot hoops?"

"Do you?" he said.

"I showed you how to play soccer," she said. "Now you can teach me how to be a basketball player."

"That seems like a fair trade."

"Follow me," she said, and they went outside through the back of the house, across a lawn even longer and wider than the Lawtons', to an even better outdoor basketball court.

Full court. More lights around it. It even had small bleachers with about five rows of seats surrounding it.

"You've got to be kidding me," Jayson said.

"My dopey brother and his friends have the best pickup games in town here in the summer," she said. "He always makes sure they have eleven guys."

"Why eleven?"

"So there's always a guy sitting out to work the scoreboard."

Scoreboard.

It turned out Zoe wasn't bad at basketball, no shocker there. After a few minutes of watching her shoot and dribble and move around, Jayson asked why she didn't play on the team at Belmont.

"During basketball season I ride horses," she said.

"You ride *horses*?"

"Jump them, too," she said. "You should come watch me sometime."

"I play H-O-R-S-E," Jayson said. "That's good enough for me."

They shot around. Jayson showed her how to put more spin on her shots. After a while, he suggested that they play one-on-one and make another bet.

"Nope," she said.

"Why not?"

"Because I'm not letting you sucker me the way I suckered you. I'm smarter than that."

He let that one go, grinning. "How about if we play without a bet, and I can only shoot left-handed?"

"Deal."

She started off with the ball, and Jayson figured he would go easy on her. He gave her an open layup on the first play to put her up by one.

On the next play, Jayson dribbled, trying to get fancy and show off, crossing from left to right, then paused when Zoe pointed somewhere far off and said, "*What* is that over there?"

Jayson wheeled around to take a look in the direction that she was pointing . . . and in that split second, Zoe swiped the ball out of his grasp, drove to the hoop, and laid it in once more.

"So you're gonna play it like that, huh?" he said.

He ended up beating her, even though she made a surprisingly good game of it. When they finished, they went and sat down in the first row of the bleachers. The sun had gone down and the air was cooler, which felt good to him after Zoe had made him work up a sweat.

"You guys were great today," he said.

"We had to be," she said. "In the end all I kept thinking about was how I would have felt watching the other team holding up that trophy at the end."

"I hate to lose, too."

"I can tell," she said.

"Well, I wasn't trying all that hard just now," he teased.

"Hard enough."

Then they sat there in silence. Not the kind of forced silence he'd get when he was with Ms. Moretti, or even with Mrs. Lawton on the ride over here. Just something that felt natural. Like they were sharing the silence together, which made it okay.

He liked that about her. She wasn't always trying to get him to talk. Or share. Or get inside his head. Usually he had enough trouble figuring out what was going on inside there himself, without trying to explain it to another person.

But he spoke first.

"It still feels strange being here," he said.

It just came out of him, like a door had suddenly opened.

"Here meaning my house?" she said. "On this court?"

"Here meaning everything," Jayson said. "Your big house, basketball court. Even living with the Lawtons and going to Belmont. I just never imagined I'd end up in a place like this."

Zoe said, "The way I look at it, Jayson, where you are is where you're supposed to be."

He wanted to ask her why *she* wanted him to be here, at this house, on this court. If she liked him for who he *really* was, or some person she imagined him to be. But he didn't. He knew that if he opened that door, if he started that conversation, he'd have to ask her how much she knew about him.

"It's only been a couple of weeks," she said. "Nobody's saying you ought to feel like you've been at Belmont forever."

She turned now and smiled at him. "But how the heck *did* you get here?"

There it was. The question he'd been dreading.

"Well . . . what have you heard?"

"What everybody has pretty much heard," she said. "Your mom passed away. You ended up on your own. Then you came to live with the Lawtons."

He forced a smile. "That's pretty much it."

Zoe punched him in the arm. "No it is not!" she said. "I mean, what was it like, living on your own? Weren't you scared?"

"Sometimes. I guess. You get used to it."

She was staring at him. "You don't have to talk about it if you don't want to."

"Even though you brought it up?"

"Well," Zoe said, "there is *that*."

"Did you invite me over just to find out stuff about me?"

He was sorry as soon as he said it. But then, he was getting used to feeling that way about things he said lately. He saw the same look on Zoe's face now that he did sometimes on Mrs. Lawton's when he'd said something to hurt her feelings.

"No," she said in a quiet voice. "I invited you over because I like hanging out with you."

"Okay," he said. Then he added, "I like hanging with you too, by the way."

There was another silence, not as long as the one before. Then Zoe said, "What would have happened to you if you hadn't ended up with the Lawtons?"

"I probably would have ended up at some kind of group home," he said. "Like a small orphanage. That's what Ms. Moretti, my caseworker, told me."

"Is she nice, this Ms. Moretti?"

"Really nice," he said, surprised at how fast that came out of him.

"She's the one who found you?"

"Pretty much."

It wasn't a lie, but it wasn't the truth, either. Maybe someday he'd tell her the whole story. Or she'd find out on her own. She just wasn't going to get it from him, not today.

"It was hard living on my own, but I got by," he said.

That much was the truth.

"What about you?" Jayson said, deciding it was time to change the subject. "It's not like I know a whole lot about you."

"Me?" she said. "Oh, there's not much to know. I'm basically supposed to play the part of Miss Perfect."

"That doesn't sound like much fun," he said.

"Oh, it could be worse," she said. "It's just how my folks, especially my mom, look at me. Perfect student, daughter, sister, rider, soccer player. Like that."

"That was never a problem for me," Jayson said. "Nobody's ever looked at me that way."

"You're lucky, then," she said. "One of the reasons I like hanging out with you is that *you* don't expect me to be Miss Perfect, so I don't have to worry about letting you down."

"Same," he said.

Zoe stood up. "Let's go get a snack."

"A snack would be great," he said, happy for an excuse to end the serious talk, at least for now.

He was hungry again. It still felt weird being able to eat a snack *any time* he wanted to. Still felt weird that he didn't go to sleep hungry every night.

They were in the kitchen, Zoe having gotten them Snapples and cookies, when they heard her mom calling out to her.

"I'm in here, Mom," she said.

Mrs. Montgomery looked like a taller, older version of Zoe, and she was already talking to Zoe as she walked into the kitchen, carrying a couple of shopping bags.

She stopped when she saw that Zoe wasn't alone.

"Oh," she said. "I didn't know we had a guest."

Mrs. Montgomery was smiling, but Jayson had the idea that she didn't mean it, and didn't like being surprised this way.

"You didn't tell me you were inviting somebody over, sweetheart."

"I told you after the game, Mom," Zoe said, looking a little embarrassed.

"I must not have been paying attention."

"This is Jayson Barnes, from school."

Mrs. Montgomery put the bags down on the counter in the middle of the kitchen, came around the counter, and put out her hand for Jayson to shake.

He knew enough about manners to get up out of his chair,

look her in the eye, and try to match her firm handshake. Ms. Moretti always shook Jayson's hand when she came over to the house, and she was the one who'd told him to stop looking down at the floor like shaking somebody's hand was a chore, so people wouldn't think he was rude.

"I'm Zoe's mom," she said.

"Very nice to meet you," Jayson said.

"You're the new boy, right?" she said. "Living with the Lawtons?"

"Yes, ma'am. Mrs. Lawton said she knew you."

"Carol and I do know each other," Mrs. Montgomery said.

She looked down at Zoe. "So what have you and your friend been up to?"

"Jayson was teaching me how to play basketball."

Even after just a couple of minutes, Jayson could see that the Zoe he knew acted differently around her mom.

"We just came in to get a snack," Zoe said.

Mrs. Montgomery made a big show of looking at her watch.

"Well," she said, "Jayson can have a snack. But you've already had pizza and you know we're having an early supper, young lady."

"Mom," Zoe said.

"Don't *Mom* me," she said. "I have a nice dinner planned and you are not going to spoil yours with cookies less than an hour before."

She turned back to Jayson now. "So how are you enjoying life on this side of Moreland?"

"It's been fine," he said.

He was already wondering how much *she* knew about him.

"It must be quite an adjustment," she said. "Zoe told me where you were living before the Lawtons took . . . before you came to live with Tom and Carol."

"I'm figuring it out," he said, adding, "with Zoe's help."

"The Lawtons are wonderful people," she said. "I don't know *how* they do it."

"Me neither."

There was an awkward pause, Jayson sure that Zoe felt it as much as he did.

"Well," Mrs. Montgomery said to Zoe finally, "I'll wait until later to show you the cute things I bought you."

Jayson said, "I should call Mrs. Lawton and tell her it's time to come get me."

"You didn't even eat any cookies," Zoe said, looking upset again.

"It's okay. I just remembered that Mrs. Lawton is cooking a big dinner tonight."

"I'll probably be upstairs when Carol comes," Mrs. Montgomery said. "Please tell her I said hi. And Jayson," she added with a fake smile, "it was a *pleasure* to meet you."

She gathered up the two shopping bags and left the room.

Jayson whipped out his phone to call Mrs. Lawton.

Wishing he could run away from Zoe's house and back to the other side of town, where he belonged.

THE SECOND HOME GAME FOR Belmont took place the following Saturday. But it wasn't just any home game, at least not for Jayson. It almost felt more like an away game.

This one was Belmont against Moreland East.

New school vs. old school. New team vs. old team.

New life vs. his old one.

He'd been thinking about it for weeks, having dreams about matching up against Tyrese, Shabazz, and the rest of his boys, but it was no longer just a thought in his mind anymore. It was real life, and game day had come.

His old team was now just another team he had to beat, the best team in the league, even without him at point guard.

It didn't mean Belmont wasn't good enough to beat the Mavericks. It didn't mean that by the end of the year, Belmont wouldn't be the best team in the league. But that was a long way off, and if they were going to reach that point, they would need to improve a lot throughout the season.

He wasn't sure in his heart—looking at the matchups, the

only player who really knew the skills and weaknesses of both teams—how they could beat the Mavericks *today*.

He and Tyrese had been talking about the game all week. Constantly texting and emailing each other. Chirping every chance they got. Each of them telling the other how the game was going to play out. Each of them saying that the other's team had *no* chance against his.

Most of the bragging was coming from Tyrese.

"Tell you what," Tyrese said on the telephone the night before. "You're gonna be so happy to see me and Shabazz that it won't hurt so bad when we put a whuppin' on you tomorrow."

"We'll see about that," Jayson had said. "I hear you're down a pretty big piece this season at point guard."

"Should send you the stat sheets, dude. Lil' Duane has been ripping it up the first couple of games."

Duane Wright had taken over Jayson's spot playing the point for Coach Rankin and the Mavericks.

"Kid is *niiiiiiiiice*," Tyrese had said. "Can hardly even tell that you're not around anymore."

"Then I guess I'll need to remind you tomorrow what it's like when I *am* around."

"Looking forward to it. And Snap, don't worry. We'll be nice to you when it's over and only one of us is still unbeaten."

"We'll see."

Jayson had tried to watch the Clippers–Warriors game on TV after he hung up, Chris Paul and Steph Curry getting after each other. But he couldn't pay attention to the game.

All he kept thinking about was his game against his old team.

As weird as it was going to feel, as much as he'd been trying to imagine what it was going to be like seeing them warming up at the other end of the court, then going toe-to-toe against Tyrese and Shabazz, one thing still mattered to him above all else: winning. He still hated losing as much as ever.

And this time, it was personal.

He thought about what Zoe had said about her championship game, what had pushed her most, and decided he didn't want to see the smug look on Tyrese's face if Moreland East won.

Jayson made sure Mrs. Lawton drove him to the gym early. He wanted to be there before Tyrese and the rest of the Mavericks showed up, wanted to be on the court when they came through the door. He still didn't feel as if the Belmont court was really his. But he wanted to make his old teammates think he did.

The game was set to start at one. Tyrese came strutting through the door at 12:15. Jayson used to tell Tyrese that he could strut sitting down. There was a big smile on his face, his eyes immediately searching for Jayson, spotting him at the opposite end of the court.

Shabazz walked in behind Tyrese, and said something to him as he pointed toward Jayson, who was shooting around with the rest of the Bobcats.

Get this over with, Jayson told himself.

He knew he was happy to see them, especially Ty, whom he hadn't seen since he ran away from the Lawtons to the Pines. But this wasn't a reunion. It was a competition both teams wanted to win. Badly.

"Those your boys?" Bryan Campbell asked.

"Not today," Jayson said as he tossed Bryan the ball, then jogged toward the visitors' bench. Like he was acting as the welcoming committee at Belmont.

Tyrese grabbed Jayson's hand and pulled him in for a chest bump. "This place is so fancy I thought I might have to wipe my shoes off before they touched the court."

"You mean before we wipe the floor with you?" Jayson said, grinning at him.

"Keep dreamin', son," Ty said.

Jason greeted the rest of the guys on his old team.

"Dude," Shabazz said, "it'll be weird playing *against* you today. But I know you're gonna bring it."

"Won't be the first time," Jayson replied. "It'll be like we're playing on different teams at the Jeff. And you know I've *brought* it in those games."

Shabazz smiled, clearly thinking about the time that Jayson had gotten in his face in a heated matchup.

Jayson nodded at Duane Wright, the starting point guard who'd taken his place, the guy he'd be guarding today.

Then Coach Rankin came over and gave Jayson a hug. "How's it going, kid?"

"It's taken some getting used to. Been a little weird," he said. "Gonna be even weirder playing against you."

Coach said, "Gonna be weird for us, too. We still feel like you're one of us."

"Not today, Coach."

Jayson turned away then, knowing his teammates on the Bobcats were all watching him, not wanting to linger too long. He walked back toward his new team.

When he was back with the rest of the Bobcats, Cameron Speeth came over and put out a fist and Jayson lightly touched it with his own.

"You must be feeling like a guy who got traded, playing against his old team for the first time," Cameron said.

"Something like that."

"I just want you to know we got your back today. You don't have to do it all yourself."

Jayson nodded. "Gonna need all the help I can get."

"We have as good a shot as they do," Cameron said. "And no matter how happy they look, I'm sure they're wishing you were standing on their side of the court."

Jayson looked over at his old team once more, and noticed Tyrese and Shabazz were staring at him.

When the Bobcats were in the huddle, right before the game was going to start, Coach Rooney said, "You boys know why I love this game?"

He didn't wait for any of them to respond.

"Because it's all about matchups. The team with the most

heart, the team that wants it the most, is the team that comes out on top." He looked around, taking them all in. "So I have a question for you: How badly do you want it?"

Jayson wanted it more than any player in the gym.

His teammates looked like they wanted it, too. Wanted to show they could run with the big dogs.

"You know where we are?" Bryan said. "Our house."

"Our house," Brandon Carr said, and then they were all jumping up and down and yelling, *"Our house! Our house!"*

As they walked out onto the court, Jayson looked up into the stands to where Mr. and Mrs. Lawton were sitting. They were both looking right at him. He put up his hand in a quick wave. Mrs. Lawton smiled and waved back.

Then Tyrese, Shabazz, and the rest of the Mavericks walked out too, smiles gone, no longer talking trash.

Looking like *they* wanted it, too.

21

JAYSON KEPT TELLING HIMSELF HE was back at the Jeff, playing against Tyrese and Shabazz like he had plenty of times in pickup games. He'd always gone at them hard, because if your team won, you got to stay on the court.

This was his court now, whether he'd chosen it or not.

The Mavericks came out hot, mostly because of Tyrese. Jayson had told Marty Samuels where Tyrese liked to shoot from, and warned him that the Mavericks would set screens for Tyrese all over the court. But warnings weren't enough to make that matchup even. Jayson could see after the first couple of minutes that Marty didn't have the quickness to keep up with Tyrese. If Jayson had been coaching, he would have subbed in Bryan first chance he got. But he wasn't coaching. And that wasn't Coach Rooney's style, to give somebody a quick hook that way. He liked to show confidence in his players. So Ty just went off in the first quarter, making four of his team's first five baskets, all from the outside, loving every minute of it.

There was a small group of parents behind the Moreland

East bench, including Tyrese's mom, but Jayson knew Tyrese wasn't focused on her or anyone else in the crowd. He was focused on one person in the gym: Jayson.

"You guys can't guard me," he said to Jayson after his last outside shot, the longest one yet.

Tyrese wasn't the only problem for the Bobcats. On defense, Shabazz was chasing Cameron all over the court, denying him the ball, blowing up screens, even blocking one of Cameron's shots about ten rows up into the seats. Shutting him down.

It was 14–2, Moreland East, when Coach Rooney finally called a time-out and subbed in Bryan for Marty, who looked gassed already from trying to keep up with Tyrese Rice.

"Everybody take some deep breaths," Coach said. "They're making their shots, we're missing ours. And guess what? If they keep making shots like this, we're gonna lose. But they're not going to. We're going to get stops on D and make our plays on offense. Move the ball around and play our game. Sound like a plan?"

They nodded.

Coach focused in on Jayson. "Don't force anything. Create space and find your opportunities."

"One basket at a time," Jayson said.

"That's what I'm talking about."

So far, it looked like the Mavericks didn't miss Jayson at all. Duane Wright, their point guard, wasn't outplaying Jayson—that wasn't the problem. The problem was that Jayson wasn't outplaying *him*. Jayson left the huddle, telling himself that was about to change, that he was ready to show his boys on his old team just what they were missing.

"I *told* you how it was gonna go," Tyrese said, just loud enough for Jayson to hear. "Been telling you all week. You should've listened."

Jayson started walking away from him.

"What," Tyrese said, trying to walk alongside Jayson, "you don't want to talk to me?"

Jayson turned and said, "Got a game to win."

First play out of the time-out, Jayson got into the lane, drew Tyrese toward him, sold the idea that he was going to shoot it himself, but kicked it to Bryan at the last second. Bryan made his first basket of the game, a wide-open fifteen footer.

One basket at a time.

At the other end of the court, Jayson snuck in on Tyrese's blind side just as Tyrese was settling in to shoot at his sweet spot, stole the ball from him, and took it himself, beating everybody down the court for a layup.

Jayson hustled back to the other end of the court, starting to get back into rhythm. And so were the rest of the Bobcats. With Phil's hand in his face, Ray Bretton missed. Cameron boxed out Shabazz for the rebound, passed it off to Jayson, who threw a football pass right back to Cameron, who was already under the basket, running his butt off, Shabazz trailing behind. Just like that, the lead was cut to 14–8.

With Bryan playing well against Tyrese and Cameron

holding his own now against Shabazz, looking more confident, the Bobcats came all the way back to tie the game by the end of the first half.

Second half coming. New game starting.

The game was still tied at the end of the third quarter. Jayson had been working Duane Wright and was clearly the stronger player of the two, finding his teammates on any open looks he could. There hadn't been many, but the Mavericks hadn't had many themselves, both teams D'ing up like they were playing in the county finals.

"We got this," Coach Rooney said to them in the huddle before the start of the fourth. "As well as we've played since we got behind early, I still don't believe we've played our best basketball. We've got the momentum now. So let's do this, boys. Let's forget about how this game started and finish off strong."

Jayson always felt as if Coach was speaking directly to him, as if he trusted Jayson to take the game in his hands and make something happen.

As they walked back out on the court, he could see Tyrese, still smiling, heading straight for him while the refs toweled off a wet spot on the court.

Tyrese hadn't been talking as much smack in the second half, considering how the game had been going. Jayson understood, because he'd seen it before, plenty of times. For all the strut and smiling and talk, Ty wanted this game as much as Jayson did.

"We let you stay in the game for a while there," Ty said, "but now it's time for the big boys to take over."

"We'll see," Jayson said.

"Just hope you don't wish that you were back with the Mavs when it's all said and done."

It was 35–35 at the start of the fourth quarter.

Brandon and Cameron were both in the game, Coach having decided to play his two bigs because he liked the matchups better. It turned out to be a good decision. Jayson knocked away Duane's first pass of the quarter, beat everybody to the ball, and threw it to a streaking Brandon Carr for a layup.

But Marty Samuels was back in the game and back on Tyrese, as bad an idea now as it had been at the start. Coach wanted to keep showing confidence in Marty, but unfortunately, that confidence didn't seem to be helping him very much.

Tyrese made three straight shots, beating Marty off the dribble twice for a couple layups. Mavericks by four.

Jayson came right back, dribbled up the court, crossed up Duane, and answered Tyrese with a rare three-pointer, Duane giving him way too much space, Jayson deciding to make him pay.

Mavericks by one.

The Bobcats and Mavericks kept on trading baskets into the last four minutes. After Tyrese scored his fifth straight basket for the Bobcats, Coach swapped Bryan for Marty again.

When he was back in the game, Bryan came over and said to Jayson, "I can shut this guy down."

Meaning Tyrese.

"Don't tell me," Jayson said. "Show me."

Bryan *did* show him. Tyrese drove to the hoop on the next play, thinking he was cruising for a score, no problem. But there was Bryan Campbell elevating as Jayson had never seen him to block the shot into the seats.

The game was tied with three minutes left. Coach Rankin called a time-out. When the Mavericks walked back onto the court, Tyrese came over to guard Jayson, Duane Wright on Bryan.

"Okay, Snap," Tyrese said to Jayson, not smiling now. "Let's do this."

Jayson said nothing. Just walked away.

He came down, dribbling too much, not even calling a play, wanting to make a statement to Tyrese right here and right now. But Tyrese stayed with him. Jayson finally started a drive, stopped himself ten feet from the basket even though he was going full speed, pump-faked to get Ty in the air, and made a jumper over him. Bobcats by two.

He wanted in the worst way to cover Tyrese, but that wasn't his call, so Bryan was still on him. Not looking to get blocked again, Tyrese came down the court, keeping his distance from Bryan, who failed to get a hand in his face, and Ty made a fadeaway jumper to tie the game once again.

Jayson forced a shot, trying to show Ty up. Then Ty fed Shabazz for a finger roll.

Mavericks by two.

Next possession for the 'Cats, Jayson had a really good look at Cameron, who'd lost Shabazz on a switch, but he decided to drive himself, and ended up putting the ball up too hard and too high over Tyrese, who got the rebound. Tyrese threw a perfect long pass to Shabazz, who'd run down to the other side of the court as soon as Tyrese had snagged the board.

Minute and a half left, Mavericks up by four.

Ty stayed on Jayson, but Brandon Carr set a hard, legal screen on him, then rolled off, cutting to the hoop, waving for the ball. But at the last second, Jayson saw a wide-open Bryan standing behind the arc, and Duane coming out to double Jayson. Jayson passed it off to Bryan, who nailed the three to cut the lead down to a point.

For the first time, Jayson realized how loud Belmont's gym had become.

The Mavericks came down and cleared out so that Shabazz could go one-on-one against Cameron. Jayson knew exactly what Shabazz was going to do: He was going to back him down if he could, use his size to post up, turn around, and take a hook from a foot away. Cameron was long, no doubt, but Shabazz was just a little bit longer.

At just the right moment, Jayson ran right at him, thinking if he couldn't get the ball he could at least rush him. But he was a step late. Shabazz had just enough of an angle to bank his shot home, and the Mavericks' lead was back to three.

Thirty seconds left.

Jayson didn't waste any time, came right at Tyrese, managed to get a step on him, and got fouled. He made both free throws, the ball rolling around the rim twice on the second one before deciding to drop through the net. The Belmont fans turned up the volume.

Mavericks 51, Bobcats 50.

Coach didn't call time, just told them to foul. Rashard fouled Ray Bretton as soon as he touched the ball, and Jayson knew Duane had made a mistake by even throwing Ray the ball. Ray was one of the worst free-throw shooters on Moreland East, especially late in games.

One-and-one. If he made the first, he would shoot a second. If he missed, the ball was up for grabs.

Ray missed, Cameron came down with the ball. Now Coach called time-out.

Twenty-two seconds showing on the clock.

The Bobcats could run down the clock and take the last shot if they wanted, but if they missed, the game was over. Their best chance was a quick score, then one stop on defense would win the game for them.

"Get set as quickly as you can," Coach said to Jayson. "Cameron, don't waste any time, come right up and set a screen. Then we take the first good shot we get."

He smiled. He always told them that moments like this were the ones you played for in sports.

"Run the new play," Coach said to Jayson.

"Got it," Jayson said.

Then Coach put his hand out. They put theirs on top of his. In a quiet voice, Coach said, "Our house."

"Long way from the Jeff," Tyrese said when he checked up on Jayson.

"Court doesn't matter," Jayson said.

"Got that right. Gonna take more than some fancy court and fancy new sneakers to beat us, Snap."

As he walked back out onto the court, Jayson looked up into the crowd to where the Lawtons were standing, along with the rest of the Belmont fans. Zoe and her friends were a couple of rows in front.

The ref came over and handed Bryan the ball. He inbounded to Jayson, who dribbled toward the top of the key, angling to his left, as Cameron ran up from the low block to set the pick that Coach Rooney called their "key to the ignition," the pick that started things in motion.

But then Brandon came running up behind Cameron, the new play that Coach had been talking about, setting a back screen for Cameron as Cameron was putting a body on Tyrese.

It all seemed to happen at once: Cameron rolling toward the basket, Shabazz running into Brandon, Shabazz falling a step behind Cameron as the Bobcats' big man made his move to the basket.

But Jayson was open, too, Tyrese having gotten lost in all the traffic of the double screen.

Ten seconds left.

Time to make his move.

Cameron had his long left arm in the air, waving for the ball, his eyes wide, looking right at Jayson.

But in that moment, Jayson felt like it was him against Moreland East. He was going to show them exactly what they were missing.

He found a clear path to the basket, pictured in his mind the layup that was going to win the game for the Bobcats.

And never saw Shabazz coming from his left.

The ball had barely left his hands when Shabazz not only blocked it, but blocked it straight at Tyrese, who caught the ball and dribbled toward the Mavericks' basket.

Jayson chased after Tyrese, hoping he might have a chance to foul before time expired. But Ty cut away from the basket—*somebody* making the right decision in these last few seconds—and there was nothing Jayson could do but watch as time ran out and the Mavericks won the game.

While Tyrese and the Mavericks celebrated, Jayson turned and saw Cameron standing next to him.

"Not that it mattered to you," Cameron said. "But I was open."

22

IT WASN'T JUST THAT CAMERON had been open on the last play, Jayson knew. Bryan had been open, too, about ten feet from the basket with nobody near him, because all the Moreland East players had been chasing Jayson and Cameron.

It bothered Jayson as much as losing the game: The play had worked exactly the way it was supposed to. But he'd been the one to blow it up.

The kid who prided himself on always making the right play, always finding the open man on a fast break, had picked that moment to throw up a hero shot. One that barely left his hand.

He made a good show of being happy for Tyrese, Shabazz, and the others, not wanting to show weakness, even now. As weak as his shot had been.

"You got me good," he said to Shabazz.

"Got lucky, is all," Shabazz said, ducking his head. He'd always been more comfortable talking about anybody's game except his own.

"How'd you know I was shooting and not passing?" Jayson said, curious, really wanting to know.

"I didn't know for sure," Shabazz said. "But you were feelin' it down the stretch, pretty much took over the game. And I thought you'd want to be the one that sealed the deal against your old boys."

Jayson could see his teammates watching him from their bench while he gave props to his old friends—and former team.

"I should've passed," Jayson said to Tyrese and Shabazz. "My center was wide open."

"Even LeBron makes the wrong play sometimes," Ty said.

"Usually it's because he's being too unselfish," Jayson said. "With me just now, it was the other way around."

Tyrese asked if he wanted to come back to the east side with him and Shabazz, and Jayson knew it would have been the first time back there since Mrs. Lawton had tracked him down at the Pines. Tyrese said they could get a game going at the Jeff later.

"Be like old times," he said.

"I can't," Jayson said.

"Can't or don't want to?" Tyrese said.

He put on his smile as he said it, but Jayson could tell he wasn't joking. He could always tell with Tyrese by checking his eyes, to see if they were smiling, too.

"It's not like that," Jayson said. "I'm just tired, is all."

"Never used to get tired before," Tyrese said.

Behind Tyrese, up in the stands, Jayson could see Zoe waving at him to come over.

"Sorry, man, but I gotta bounce right now," Jayson said. "I'll check you later."

Shabazz turned to Tyrese and said, "First time in history the boy passed up a game at the Jeff."

Tyrese was watching Jayson's eyes, the way he did during a game. He turned and followed them all the way over to Zoe.

Tyrese said, "Maybe it's not as bad over here as you've been letting on."

"C'mon, man," Jayson said. "You know I'm being straight with you."

"Nah, I think I get it now," Tyrese said.

Without another word, they turned their backs on him and headed for the door, Jayson feeling one last time as if he were caught between his old team and his new one.

When Jayson walked over to Zoe, she said, "That guy swatted you away like that Weston goalie kept doing to me."

"Thanks," he said. "That makes me feel a lot better."

"C'mon, you know I'm just joking," she said. "You nearly won the game for your team."

"Tried to win it for *myself*, but lost it for my team in the end," he said. "The difference between our games is that you were supposed to take the final shot, but I should've passed."

"It was one game," she said.

"Every game matters. Some more than others."

"You'll get them next time."

He kept quiet, mostly because he didn't know what to say.

"I'm getting nowhere with my pep talk."

"I'm not in the mood," he said.

"Listen," she said. "I've got to go to the mall with my mom."

"You're telling me this . . . why?"

"Because, Dr. Doom, I thought that if I got back in time, we could hang out at my house later."

"Call me when you're done."

"Only if you promise to be in a better mood."

"No promises."

"I don't know," she said, fun in her eyes. "I think it's hard for you to stay in a bad mood around me."

At that moment, Mrs. Montgomery walked into the gym and gave Zoe a look that said it was time to go, not even looking at Jayson.

"I better get going," Zoe said.

She never called. Jayson was actually glad. He didn't want to be with anybody today, not even her. He wanted to be alone.

It was always easier that way.

It was near dinnertime at the Lawtons', but Jayson was out on their basketball court, where he'd been since he'd gotten home.

Working on his game. Still thinking about the one he'd just played, breaking it down possession by possession. Almost like he was playing against Moreland East all over again.

Trying to find one more bucket for his team.

He knew he should've passed the ball in that situation. That was his game. It was who he was, the player he prided himself on being. But by the time the Bobcats got the ball at the end, he'd turned into somebody else: a point guard who'd made the whole game about himself and not his team, someone who'd tried to prove some kind of point, lost sight of the bigger picture in the process.

But *who* had he been trying to prove a point to?

His old team? His new one? Himself?

He banged a line-drive shot off the side of the rim and started to chase after the ball, until he saw that Mrs. Lawton had already picked it up for him. He'd been so focused on his shooting—and replaying the game in his mind—that he hadn't even noticed her walk outside.

She stepped onto the court and threw him a perfect two-handed bounce pass, the ball spinning into his hands with some nice topspin.

It was a pass from somebody who knew what she was doing with a basketball in her hands.

"You *played*?" he said.

"Don't sound so shocked."

"You never said anything."

"You never asked," she said. "And I figured that basketball was something you wanted to work on alone."

She was right about that, but he was still surprised that she'd never told him she'd been a player. "Did you play on school teams?"

"I was a tall east-side girl who was a decent athlete," she said. "It was practically my duty." She grinned. "Ended up being a starter at Moreland East in high school."

"I can't believe you never told me."

"You never seem to want to watch Duke games with Tom," she said, "so I didn't think you'd be interested in an old lady's basketball past."

Jayson cocked his head. "Were you any good?"

"Good enough to be a starter, but I was never a star like you."

"Yeah," he said, "I was a *total star* at the end of the game today."

"My high school coach used to tell me it's never just one play that decides a basketball game."

"Well, it felt like that to me. And it'll be the play that everyone remembers."

"It was a hard day for you," she said. "You put too much pressure on yourself to show your new teammates that you belonged on that court. That you could be the leader of the Bobcats."

"Well, I don't know that I belong anywhere. My teammates probably don't want to speak to me right now, and Tyrese and Shabazz think I big-timed them." He sighed loudly. "I wanted that win so badly."

"Wanting to win that badly," she said, "is part of what makes you the great player you are. Part of what makes you deserve to be on that court."

He didn't feel so great at that moment, standing there with

Mrs. Lawton. But at least he always had basketball to distract him. Even if he needed to use it to distract himself from *more* basketball.

"You want to take a couple of shots?" he said. "Show me what you've got?"

"My playing days are over," she said, smiling at him. "Why don't I just feed the ball to you?"

"Isn't it getting close to supper?"

"Supper can wait."

She rebounded for him over the next few minutes while he moved around the perimeter and took outside shots. After each shot, Jayson watched her and thought that she did have the instincts of a good athlete. She made left-handed passes and right-handed passes, and just about all of them seemed to hit him in stride, so all he had to do was catch and shoot. Nothing fancy, just good old mechanics. She kept dishing him the ball while neither one of them said anything.

But through the silence, for some reason he was starting to feel more relaxed than when he'd been out here by himself.

"I used to do this with Isaiah when he'd let me. He'd come out here after a tough loss and do exactly what you've been doing, sometimes into the night. Almost like he was trying to *sweat* the bad plays out of himself."

"I understand that. Basketball has always been the only thing that I could really depend on."

Mrs. Lawton gave him a sad smile. "Well, you can depend on Tom and me, too. Even if we don't always see eye to eye.

Sometimes, kids want to live their life one way, but their parents see differently."

"Did that happen with Isaiah?" Jayson asked. Whatever was going on between the Lawtons and their son wasn't really any of his business, he knew, but Mrs. Lawton had already started the conversation.

"Something like that."

"Where is he, anyway?"

"He's taking some time away. Trying to figure out his life. I think about him every day. Hope beyond hope that he's okay, and that once he's done with all that figuring out, he'll come back home. Home is important. Sometimes we figure that out later rather than sooner."

Mrs. Lawton didn't seem to want to say any more about the situation, so Jayson dropped it.

He knew he had been out on the Lawtons' court for hours, and felt like he'd been winding down before Mrs. Lawton came outside. But now he was in no rush to go back into the house. Mrs. Lawton didn't seem to be, either.

"C'mon," he said finally, "you've got to take a couple of shots. I played ball with you, now it's your turn."

She shrugged and held her hands out, calling for a pass. He tossed the ball to her and she took a couple of dribbles.

"Take a few from the outside," he said.

"What, a sister can't warm up?"

She hit a couple layups and then ran out to the right of the foul line, clapped her hands, and said, "Feed me, I'm open."

Now Jayson threw her a perfect bounce pass, one she caught chest-high. Then she let her shot go. He thought for a moment that she'd released it too low, almost like she was shooting the ball off her right hip.

But the shot dropped softly through the hoop. Nothing but net.

"Great," he said. "*Now* I get my last assist of the day."

"Better late than never," she said.

When he made a motion like he was going to pass her the ball again, she shook her head.

"Nope, I'm quitting while I'm ahead. One and done. But you can shoot a little more if you want to. I'm happy to keep feeding you."

"I'll bet you never expected this to be part of your job when you took me in," he said.

She shook her head. "It's not a job, Jayson. Tom and I couldn't be happier to have you in our lives."

"Even when I break your stuff?"

Mrs. Lawton sighed. "Well, now that you mention it, maybe we *should* send you back."

She caught Jayson's eye and winked.

They sat down in the cool grass, facing each other, as the sun went down and the fall day began to turn into night. Mrs. Lawton sat cross-legged. Jayson sat with the basketball in the grass between his legs.

"Today was a disaster," he said to her. "I could've at least played my game, played smart. I was the reason we lost."

"You could look at it that way. But you were also the

reason your team came back and had a chance to win with the last shot," she said. "And this was on a day when you had to feel like you were playing on both teams. Trying to prove something to both teams. And prove to yourself that you could take all that on and still come out a winner. That's an awful lot to handle, even for someone who can play basketball the way you can."

"I still should've passed," Jayson said to her.

She smiled. "Heck, even people in outer space know that."

Jayson couldn't help himself or stop himself. He laughed.

THERE WERE TWO GAMES THE next week, one against Moreland West, and a rematch against Karsten, both away games.

Belmont won them both. Put the loss against Moreland East in the past. At least for now.

If anything, Jayson over-passed in both games, as if wanting to show his teammates—maybe *needing* to show them—that he wasn't the selfish player he'd been at the end of the Moreland East game.

He took just six shots against Moreland West and made four of them. Then he took seven against Karsten and hit four. He scored less than ten points in both games. Instead, he played to his strengths, handing off the ball to Cameron Speeth, who carried the scoring load, scoring twenty points in both games, hitting his shots from inside, outside, and on the break. Jayson would never say it to him, because he couldn't think of a way to say it without the words coming out wrong, but he'd found himself a brand new Shabazz on the court.

He didn't ignore the other guys, either. He found open looks for Bryan and Brandon and Rashard, too. But his go-to guy was his big man. Cameron was a point guard's dream. He was a finisher. And Jayson was letting Cameron know that *he* knew.

After the Karsten game, Coach Rooney came over to talk to Jayson. "I get what you're doing. And I know why you're doing it. I respect that. But you can't pass up open looks for the rest of the season."

"My job is to find the open man."

They had come back from Karsten in one of Belmont's small buses and were standing in front of the gym. Jayson could see the Lawtons waiting for him in their car.

"And you're doing a real good job of finding the open man," Coach said. "But when *you* are the open man, take the shot."

Somehow, Jayson had been throwing himself into basketball more than ever, especially now that he could see his team's potential. He really believed that they could make it all the way to Cameron Indoor. He was spending as much time as he could on the Lawtons' court. Mrs. Lawton even came back out to help him sometimes, but she always waited for him to ask.

It wasn't as if somebody had turned a switch and suddenly he was happy, suddenly he'd decided that he belonged at Belmont and with the Lawtons. Jayson still wasn't even sure what it meant to be happy a lot of the time.

But at least these days he wasn't going around looking to pick a fight with the world every chance he got.

"You seem . . . more relaxed," Ms. Moretti said to him during her weekly visit.

"Don't get used to it."

"Why not? Isn't that better than the way things were before?"

"It's only a matter of time until I mess up again. Or until the kids at school, their parents, my teammates and Coach find out why I *really* ended up living here."

Jayson thought about the way Mrs. Montgomery had treated him, and could only imagine what she would think if she found out the truth.

"What about your friends at school? Do you think they would look at you differently if you told them about your past?"

"I don't know," Jayson said. "Maybe. Not about to find out, though."

"I think if you ever explained it to someone like your friend Zoe, she'd understand," Ms. Moretti said.

"No way I would ever tell Zoe about that."

"If she ever did have to hear it, wouldn't you rather it come from you?"

"Zoe likes me for who I am now," he said. "Who she *thinks* I've always been. I don't see any reason to change that."

Later that day, Bryan called and asked him to meet up in town for pizza along with Cameron and Brandon. Jayson thought, *Why not?* It would be the first time he'd hung out with the guys on the team away from games or practice.

They were at a front booth at Joe's Pizza. He felt a little awkward, though the rest of the guys acted like being together outside of practice was normal. Which, he knew, it was. Somehow, after all the time they'd spent together on the court, he still didn't know how to act with his teammates off the court.

They had ordered two pepperoni pizzas, Brandon joking that one of them was for him, and were waiting for their number to be called. Jayson couldn't help it, but this was another time when he thought back to the Pines, and how many times he had to make one large pizza last for days when he was living by himself.

Cameron looked like he had something he wanted to ask, but didn't quite know how to do it. So he just came out with it straight. "Is it getting less weird for you, living with the Lawtons?"

"It's still weird," Jayson said. "But everybody's trying real hard. Even me."

"Mr. and Mrs. Lawton seem to be doing their best, showing up to all your games," Bryan said.

"Yeah, can't say they aren't doing whatever they can," Jayson said. "Now it's on me to do the same."

For some reason he didn't feel as if the guys were pressing him; they could just as easily have been recapping the Karsten game. Maybe because they were slowly becoming his boys.

"Not to be nosy here," Brandon said, grinning, "but how

did you even end up with the Lawtons? We've heard some stuff, but never from you."

He gave Brandon a fake smile. He'd been getting good at that lately. "Long story, but the short version is that someone found out that I was living by myself after my mom died. And then this woman from Child Services got involved, and she was the one who brought me to Mr. and Mrs. Lawton."

He raised his shoulders, dropped them, and said, "And now here we are."

It was at that moment that the front door to Joe's opened and a familiar-looking man walked in. Jayson couldn't remember who it was at first. But then the man turned his head, and Jayson got a good look at him.

It was Pete. The guy from Foot Locker.

JAYSON HAD WANTED TO MAKE things right at the Foot Locker. He knew Mr. Lawton had already paid for the sneakers Jayson had stolen, but he wanted to buy them with his own money. The Lawtons had given him an allowance each week, but insisted that Jayson had to earn it by doing more than simply keeping his room clean. So he cleaned out the garage, made sure the basketball court got swept, and piled the wood that Mr. Lawton would chop for the fireplace. He made it his job, every night after dinner, to clear the table, stack the dishes in the dishwasher, and clean any pots and pans that needed to be cleaned by hand.

He just wasn't ready yet, didn't have enough money saved. Even if he did have the money, he wasn't sure he was ready to face the people he'd stolen from.

But now the thing that made him most ashamed had just come walking through the door.

He pulled out his phone and casually looked down at it while he tried to figure out how he wanted to play out the situation. His coaches, teammates, and even players on the other team talked about how Jayson Barnes could always think one move ahead of everybody else on the court. He was trying like crazy to do that now.

"You expecting to hear from Zoe?" Bryan said, grinning. "You're staring at the phone like you're waiting for something to happen."

"What? No, no, nothing like that." But he kept staring at the phone like it was the most important thing he'd do all day, more important than beating Karsten earlier. "It's just that Mrs. Lawton said she was going to text me about something I had to do later."

He knew it was lame, but it was all he had at the moment.

He shot a quick look at the counter, praying that Pete wouldn't turn around and remember him, remember what he'd done. Jayson had no idea whether Pete was there to eat at the restaurant or pick up takeout.

But Jayson wasn't willing to risk the chance that Pete might come over and out him in front of his friends. He dreaded the thought of having to explain the whole situation to the guys afterward.

He briefly thought about telling them the truth. Why not? They were his teammates; he could try swearing them to secrecy, and maybe it would work. But then they'd know. And from then on they'd look at him differently. They'd smile and pretend everything was the same, but it wouldn't be. He'd be a thief in their eyes instead of just their teammate and starting point guard. And eventually one of them would tell somebody else, and that's all it would take, and before long everybody in the seventh grade would know. Including Zoe.

His head was spinning with all kinds of thoughts, some of them crazy. But the only one that mattered was this:

He had to get out of here—right now.

He took another look around. It wasn't all that crowded at Joe's, just three booths along the wall were taken, one table filled with a bunch of girls.

He heard the kid taking Pete's order say, "To stay or to go?"

"Stay. Don't want to have to reheat the best pie in the county when I get home."

That was it. Jayson reached into his pocket for his phone, like he'd just been buzzed even if they hadn't heard it, and said to the guys, "Ah, man, I was afraid of this. I gotta go. Mrs. Lawton is gonna pull up in like one minute."

"You didn't even eat yet," Bryan said. "She can't wait ten minutes?"

"I promised her," Jayson said.

He took a few dollars out of his pocket and threw the money on the table. Cameron said they'd pay for it; Jayson hadn't even eaten anything. "Nah, it's cool," Jayson said. "I'm part of the team now." He was watching Pete, still up at the counter, chatting with the cashier. Jayson was hoping to time his exit just right.

"See you guys at practice," he said.

The second Pete turned around and started looking for a place to sit while he waited for his pizza, Jayson stood up and walked away from the booth, almost bumping into Pete as he made his way to the door. "Sorry," he said as he kept moving, head down, the door nearly hitting him in the face as another customer came walking into Joe's. "Sorry."

Then he was out the door and gone, out on the sidewalk, looking down at the same sneakers he'd stolen weeks back.

Jayson waited for that same large hand to come down firmly on his shoulder.

But it never did.

When he got back, the Lawtons were in the living room. Mrs. Lawton was reading and Mr. Lawton was watching a basketball game. Mrs. Lawton put her glasses on top of her head and bookmarked her page when Jayson came in.

"You said you were going to call," she said. "Did one of the other boys' parents give you a ride?"

He was tired of making things up today, so he didn't even try.

"I walked home," he said.

Mr. Lawton muted the TV with his remote. "Jayson, that's more than a four-mile walk. Why didn't you just call?"

It was quiet in the room without the sound of the game. He checked out the screen and remembered that Kentucky was playing Kansas today.

"Jayson," Mrs. Lawton said. "Did something happen?"

"It was no big deal," he said, even though he knew it was a very big deal, at least to him.

"It was enough to make you walk home alone."

"Not as if I'm not used to being on my own."

"You want to tell us what happened?" Mr. Lawton said.

Jayson looked at Mr. and Mrs. Lawton. They were waiting for him to speak. Finally he sighed again. "The man who caught me after I stole the sneakers came into Joe's when I was there with my teammates."

Mrs. Lawton put her book down now and sat forward in her chair. "I see."

"No, you don't," he said. "You *don't* see. You don't know what it's like to feel like I'm still hiding, even though I'm living here now." He was breathing hard, just like that, taking air in and letting it out.

"What you did was wrong, Jayson," Mrs. Lawton said. "But it wasn't the crime of the century, either. Do you really think people would think so differently about you if they knew you stole a pair of sneakers so you could be like the other players on your team?"

"Yes," he said. "It was pathetic. *I* was pathetic."

"You're many things, Jayson, but never pathetic," Mrs. Lawton said.

"My friends don't really know me," he said. "They just know the made-up version, the one who lives with you."

"Well, I know the real you," she said, "whether you want to believe that or not. I think you're a good person with a good heart doing amazingly well with circumstances that would have crushed most kids your age."

He wanted to believe her. Wanted people to see him as

more than just a thief. But for now he just wanted to get out of this room, the way he'd gotten out of Joe's.

"You've got to stop being so hard on yourself," Mr. Lawton said.

"I'm just so tired of feeling like a phony, like at any minute I need to run."

"At least this time you ran home," Mrs. Lawton said.

25

THE BOBCATS KEPT WINNING, AND kept looking more like a team that could win the league every time they played. When Jayson was playing ball, he knew exactly who he was: the point guard whose role was making everybody around him better.

He wasn't seeing as much of Zoe on the weekends. Not since that awkward conversation with her mom at her house. She'd canceled on him a couple times out of the blue, which was a little weird, but he didn't think too much of it. She had mentioned that she would be doing a lot of riding and going to horse shows in the area.

He kept in touch with Tyrese and talked to him a couple of times a week. But Jayson didn't want to go back to the Jeff, and he didn't invite Tyrese over to the west side to hang with him. They were still friends, but more than ever it felt like a long-distance friendship to Jayson, the two of them living on different sides of Moreland. Jayson felt like he'd be as much of a phony going back to the old hood now as he was going to Belmont Khaki Day.

Ms. Moretti kept coming for her weekly visits and kept telling him how much "progress" she thought he was making. Sometimes Jayson would ask her how she could tell.

"You seem more relaxed," she said.

"Then I'm fooling you," he said. "I don't relax. I just keep grinding away."

"In everything?" she said. "Even with school and the friends you're making?"

"Pretty much."

"So this is just one big show; you're really not enjoying your life over here?"

"It's better than it was," Jayson said. "Isn't that enough?"

She smiled. "My goal is for you to be happy."

"Everybody seems to want that," he said. "But it's like I keep telling you—that's on me."

"Like it's another opponent you need to beat? Jayson Barnes against the world?"

"Something like that."

They left it there. It was a week before Christmas. Jayson wasn't quite sure how he felt about his first Christmas at the Lawtons'. It had never been a very big deal at the Pines, just him and his mom, usually one or two presents. The last one they'd spent together, she'd been in bed for most of the day.

Mrs. Lawton's mom had died young of cancer a long time ago, though not as young as Jayson's mom had been. She hadn't seen her father since he'd left the family when she was a little girl. Mr. Lawton's parents lived in Arizona and didn't like to fly.

Even so, Mr. and Mrs. Lawton walked around the house looking cheerful, but every once in a while, Jayson could see a sad look on their faces, and he wondered if they were thinking of their son. Isaiah had told them it was doubtful he would be coming home for the holidays. It was weird, Jayson thought, how some people would give anything to grow up in a home like Isaiah's, while others just wanted to run away. He wondered which of the two options he wanted for himself now.

He woke up at his normal time on Christmas morning. When he came downstairs, the Lawtons were waiting for him, Mrs. Lawton telling him she had been about five minutes from waking him up, since she couldn't wait any longer to open presents.

"You go first," she said, looking happier and more excited than he felt.

They had gotten him Xbox Live Gold, both the Lawtons knowing that Jayson liked playing video games more and more now. It was like a whole new world had opened up to him once he'd started playing some of Isaiah's old games. They'd also gotten him NBA 2K16, and more new clothes, even though Mrs. Lawton had sworn she wasn't getting him more new clothes.

"I couldn't help myself," she said.

Mr. and Mrs. Lawton gave each other their presents next. She had gotten him a new blazer. He gave her a new watch. When they were done thanking and hugging each other, Jayson told them to wait, ran upstairs, and came back with the two presents he'd bought for them with the money he'd been saving up from his chores—the reason he still didn't have enough money to pay for the sneakers.

He handed the first box to Mr. Lawton. Inside was the tie that Mrs. Lawton had helped him pick out. Mr. Lawton put it around his neck and tied it, even though he was still wearing his bathrobe.

"How do I look?" he said to Jayson.

"In that outfit?" Jayson said.

Mr. Lawton had a goofy smile on his face. "I think I look pretty fly."

Jayson smiled. Then, feeling a little nervous, he handed Mrs. Lawton the square box that he'd wrapped himself, even sticking one of those little Christmas bows on the top.

She grinned and started to shake it but right away Jayson said, "No!"

"Oops," she said. "Sorry."

They were all sitting on the floor next to the tree. She took off the bow and carefully unwrapped the present.

He had found the beautiful horse online. It wasn't bronze but it looked like bronze, that's what the description said. He knew it wasn't as beautiful as the one Mrs. Lawton had made herself, but it was the best he could do.

It was as close as he could come to putting her horse back together.

He had tracked the package all week, right up until it was finally delivered to the Lawtons' front door. He'd caught a break when the UPS truck showed up, because Mrs. Lawton had been out for a walk. He'd signed for it, wrapped it right away after taking a quick look, and then hidden it under his bed. Feeling in that moment as if it were as valuable as the picture of him with his mom, or his basketball trophies. Only this time, it was something he couldn't wait to give away. Something he wasn't trying to shut away in a drawer somewhere, out of view.

Mrs. Lawton didn't hold it in her hands like it was bronze—she held it like it was made of pure gold.

Her eyes filled up right away.

"I had to put it on Mr. Lawton's credit card, but I paid him exactly what it cost."

"That he did," Mr. Lawton said.

Mrs. Lawton still hadn't said anything, just sat there with the horse in her hands, staring at it.

"Anyway," Jayson said, "I hope you like it even though I know it's nowhere near as nice as the one you made."

She looked at him and said, "I don't just like it, Jayson. I love it. Thank you so much."

It wasn't her horse. But it would do. And even though the Lawtons' house still didn't feel like *his* home, on this Christmas morning it would definitely do.

AS THE BOBCATS KEPT WINNING, stringing together a streak that put their record at 8-2, so did the Moreland East Mavericks.

Jayson wasn't big into social media, even if just about everybody else was at Belmont Country Day. He wasn't on Facebook or Twitter, at least not yet, and knew as much about Instagram as he did about riding horses. There was still a big part of him that was afraid that the more he put himself out there, the more exposed he'd be.

He'd spent so much of his life hiding stuff, even at twelve, it was hard to get out of the habit.

But there were enough guys on the team who were into social media, so as soon as the Mavericks won another game, everyone else found out. Before the 'Cats took the court at Belmont to play St. Patrick's on the second Saturday in January, Bryan looked up from his phone, excited to tell everybody that Weston had just upset Moreland East. Somebody on the Weston team had already tweeted out that Tyrese had missed a shot at the buzzer to win.

"That ought to stop his chirping," Bryan said.

Jayson shook his head. "Shabazz used to say that the only thing that would be left after a nuclear attack was the sound of Tyrese's voice."

"All I know," Bryan said, "is that if we win today, we'll have the same record as East Moreland."

Everybody in the locker room knew that the rematch between the Bobcats and the Mavericks in a few weeks, in the gym at Moreland East Middle, would be the last game of the regular season for both teams.

"Gotta be honest," Cameron said. "I can't wait to beat those guys."

"Let's just focus on beating the guys we're playing today first," Jayson said.

That was all he was thinking about right now. Winning the game they were playing today.

Then, after the game, he would meet up with Zoe in town. She didn't have a horse show today; she was just riding at her barn while the Belmont–St. Patrick's game was going on.

Jayson knew all too well that the best player on St. Patrick's was a sweet-shooting forward named Derrick Bennett, who had moved away from the Jeff when his dad got a job driving for UPS. Derrick was tall and skinny and wore his hero Kevin Durant's number, 35. He was quiet; Jayson remembered that from the Jeff. But what he remembered even better was Derrick's game. Derrick could shoot over most of the kids who tried to guard him, because he was so long. But as tall as he was, he was still quick enough to drive past someone who got up too close on him.

Before the game he came over to Jayson and said, "Heard you ended up here."

"Like you ended up at St. Patrick's."

"How's it going?" Derrick asked.

"It takes some getting used to, but it's all right, I guess. How about you?"

"I miss balling at the Jeff sometimes, but it's not too bad."

"Yeah, I hear that."

They bumped fists and went back to their own benches. Jayson was smiling as he did.

Not everybody in the world wore you out with conversation.

Derrick showed early on in the game that he could wear out the Belmont Bobcats, though, no matter who tried to guard him. Coach Rooney even switched to a zone defense to see if that would slow Derrick down, but the kid kept on scoring. When the 'Cats were coming out of a time-out in the third quarter, still down ten points, Bryan said to Jayson, "I know you said that guy loves Durant, but I feel like we're going up against the real thing."

"He's only one player," Jayson said. "Better team still wins."

Following Coach's instructions, Jayson had been taking his shots today, and making most of them. But Cameron was missing easy shots that he usually made. Every player had an off game, but Jayson wished that Cameron hadn't gone cold today with Derrick playing the way he was. It was the offense the 'Cats were getting from Jayson, Rashard, and Bryan that was keeping them in the game. Barely.

It was still 38–30, St. Patrick's Pistons, with six minutes left in the game. Jayson was pretty sure Derrick had close to thirty points.

Derrick had just gotten a brief rest, but now the Pistons' coach had called time-out to get him back in there. Jayson ran off the court first, and right to Coach Rooney.

"Put me on Derrick the rest of the game," he said.

"He's six inches taller than you."

"I know," Jayson said, talking fast. "But they've been playing him up top, like a point guard, for most of the second half. Put me on him, Coach. I won't let him get around me."

Coach Rooney thought about it, but not for long. Then he smiled. "I like it. We'll play a two-two zone behind you. Cameron and Brandon down low, Rashard and Bryan in front of them. The old box-and-one. And you're the one, kid. I should've thought of it earlier."

"If it doesn't work, it's on me," Jayson said.

"Nope, it's on all of us," Coach Rooney said. "Like always."

Jayson jogged back onto the court and squared up against Derrick. The St. Patrick's star looked confused, must've been wondering why he was being defended by a point guard who barely reached his shoulders. But he didn't smile or laugh. He'd seen Jayson play at the Jeff enough times to know not to underestimate him.

And Jayson had been right: Derrick *couldn't* get around

him, at least not easily. Jayson was too quick, making Derrick really work just to get the ball past midcourt. And when he did manage to work himself down closer to the basket, there were Cameron and Brandon waiting to jam him up. He started forcing shots and missing.

The 'Cats were all over the rebounds, pushing the ball on the break every chance they got, Jayson bringing the ball down the court, dishing it to Rashard and Bryan in the corners. The momentum swung so much that even Cameron began playing like his old self down low. The new defense worked well enough to get them back in the game, at a time when falling behind even more would have been the same as losing.

With two minutes left, Jayson came down the court on a fast break, looking directly ahead like he was going straight for the hoop. Yet he had seen Derrick gaining on him out of the corner of his eye, so he threw a no-look pass to Cameron, who was trailing just a couple of steps behind, and who banked it home. All of a sudden it was 48–48, the first time the game had been tied since the score was 2–2. The only problem? Jayson was exhausted, feeling his legs get heavier and heavier, because of all the work he'd been doing against Derrick on defense. For the first time all season, the kid who never got tired *was* tired. With a minute and ten seconds left, he grabbed Derrick as Derrick started to make a move around him, a tired foul if there ever was one.

Derrick went to shoot a one-and-one. Jayson put his hands on his knees. Bryan came over to him.

"You okay?"

"Yeah."

"The reason I'm asking you," Bryan Campbell said, "is because you don't look okay."

"I got enough left to finish these guys off."

"Let the rest of us help you," Bryan said. "You can't rest on defense, but let me bring the ball up, so you can at least get a little rest on offense."

Jayson looked up and decided to trust his teammate. Let the others get his back, like Cameron had once said. "Okay."

Derrick made both free throws.

Bryan brought the ball up while Jayson jogged upcourt and went to the wing, letting Bryan take control of the offense. The rest of the Pistons were still eyeballing Jayson, like this was some kind of trick play, because Jayson had been running the offense the whole game.

Only it wasn't a trick. Cameron came up, set a pick—which got Belmont the defensive switch they wanted—then Cameron rolled off and Bryan lobbed him a pass over the top of the smaller defender. Cameron laid it in and got fouled. The old pick-and-roll, executed to perfection.

Cameron made the free throw.

Bobcats by one, first lead of the game.

Jayson was as happy as if he'd made the pass himself. With the clock ticking, he took a deep breath and picked up Derrick on a full-court press, making the St. Patrick's player use up nearly all of the ten seconds he was allowed.

Under a minute. Jayson thought Derrick looked a little tired, too. This time, Jayson wasn't going to have to foul him. Wouldn't let Derrick get past him. With Jayson jamming him up, not giving him an inch to find a lane, Derrick gave up and forced up a three-pointer, more out of frustration than anything else.

And banked the sucker home.

Jayson couldn't believe his eyes. Pure luck. But it didn't change the fact that the Pistons were now up by two, with forty-five seconds left.

As Jayson came past the 'Cats bench, he heard Coach Rooney say, "Quick two if we can get a good look."

Jayson nodded, and didn't wait for the high screen this time; instead, he put a sweet head fake on the redheaded kid who'd been guarding him the whole game, beating him cleanly off the dribble. Derrick didn't get over in time to cut him off, so Jayson blew past the whole Pistons squad for the layup that tied the game again, with thirty-eight seconds left.

The Pistons' coach couldn't call time, having used them all already. Which was fine with Jayson, who felt like he had fresh legs again after the breather. He was on Derrick again, continued to press him hard upcourt. Derrick was right-handed and hadn't tried to go hard to his left all day. Jayson knew he had Bryan behind him. He made a motion with his left hand, telling Bryan to come up out of his spot in the zone and double-team *right now.*

As Bryan charged forward, Derrick got spooked, and took his eyes off Jayson just long enough for Jayson to take the ball from him.

Not batting it away. *Taking* it, right off the kid's dribble, like he could have said, "Thank you very much." Stole it from under his nose.

With his momentum propelling him forward, Jayson headed toward the sideline. But right before he went out of bounds, he pulled up, kept dribbling the ball inbounds, and tiptoed along the sideline, making one of those quick stops he had always been able to make, no matter where his body was taking him, no matter how fast he'd been going.

He turned toward the Bobcats' basket and saw there were fifteen seconds left on the clock. He went flying up the left side of the court, Derrick the only Piston back on defense for the moment, having turned and headed to the other end of the court as soon as Jayson had made the steal.

But Bryan had done the same thing, flying alongside Jayson on the right side of the court.

Two-on-one, but not for long.

He figured he could take Derrick again, now that he had him backing up this way, even with Derrick's height advantage and his long arms.

But he'd already lost one game for his team getting a shot swatted, and he wasn't going to let that happen again. When he was even with the foul line, still coming from the left, he dropped his shoulder, like he was going to try to take it all the way to the basket.

Derrick bit.

With just enough room to work with, Jayson kept the ball on his left-hand dribble, and somehow managed to lean around Derrick to launch a perfect bounce pass into Bryan's hands for a layup.

Bobcats up by two.

Three seconds left.

The Pistons rushed down the court to get in position for the final play, no time-outs left to stop the clock. The Pistons' shooting guard inbounded the ball, threw a desperation pass the length of the court toward Derrick, whose long arms reached up to come down with the ball. But Cameron bodied his way in front of Derrick, and intercepted the ball a second before the buzzer went off.

Ballgame.

Coach Rooney was so excited he leaped off the bench and ran onto the court, hugging his players one by one. "Great steal!" he said when he got to Jayson. "Better pass."

"If Bryan doesn't pick me up," Jayson said, "it doesn't matter."

They had been a complete team today. And this time a teammate had made Jayson better.

27

MR. LAWTON WAS PLAYING GOLF. Mrs. Lawton had a lunch date in Percy with a friend she'd gone to school with at Moreland Middle, so she dropped Jayson off in town earlier than he was supposed to meet Zoe.

"What do you two plan to do?" Mrs. Lawton said in the car.

"Just eat and maybe hang out after," Jayson said. "Zoe'll probably decide."

"So Zoe calls the shots?" she asked, smiling so that Jayson knew she was joking.

"Pretty much."

"Shocker," she said. "I'm sure you'll have fun."

"I don't think she'll give me a choice," Jayson said.

Jayson looked at his phone when he got out of the car. He still had an hour before he was scheduled to meet Zoe at the Elm Street Diner, with its long counter and booths and the best burgers and shakes in the downtown area.

The sun was out and it felt more like a cool spring day than winter, with a lot of people out walking around. Jayson decided to do the same, realizing something as he headed up Main Street: He was smiling.

Thinking back on the game, he felt good about the way the team had played, the way he'd played, the way they were coming together, the way that pass had felt and the steal right before it. He felt good about playing through fatigue the way he had. You heard all the time in sports about how you were supposed to leave it all on the court. He knew he'd given every ounce of himself today. And he'd had enough left at the end to help his team win the game, after his team had helped him.

You couldn't ask for much more than that.

Main Street was a long block. He walked up one side of it and then down the other. Now that the Christmas shopping season had been over for a couple of weeks, many of the store windows had "Sale" signs in them.

He looked in some of those windows, just killing time, not recognizing anybody from school on the street. But as he walked, he couldn't help thinking about the last time he'd walked a downtown street like this, that Saturday afternoon in Percy, the one that ended up changing his whole life. He wasn't window shopping that day, just deciding about his escape route after he'd stolen the shoes.

But what if he hadn't done it?

What if he'd just chickened out that day? If he'd been too afraid to go through with it? It would've been nothing new—he'd spent so much time being afraid, living alone, even if he didn't like to admit that to himself. He'd especially been afraid of being caught and ending up in foster care. Or maybe he'd really been afraid of *not* being caught.

What if the fear of getting caught had made him change his mind, had made him just get back on a bus and head home to the Pines? How long would he have been able to stay ahead of Child Protective Services?

How long before he would've met Ms. Moretti? Would he ever have at all? Some other social worker could've found him and sent him straight to a group home.

He would've never come to live with the Lawtons.

Where would I be today? Better yet, *who* would he have become?

He'd have played a game with the Moreland East Mavericks, been out there with Tyrese and Shabazz and the rest of his boys. But after the game, what then? Back to the court at the Jeff? Back to Tyrese's apartment?

Back to his own empty apartment? Back to the hunger, and stealing peanut butter and bread to make it through the night?

He was hungry now, but that was all right; he knew he'd be eating one of those burgers soon and ordering himself a chocolate shake. It was a different kind of hunger—a temporary one that didn't take stealing to satisfy.

He decided to go to the Village Market to get a snack while he waited for Zoe, a bag of chips and a Gatorade, not looking to spoil his lunch.

He walked into the market, and this was another moment

that took him back to the life he'd been living on the east side, when he'd walk into corner stores because he had to steal to eat. He pictured himself in one of those stores now, knowing where the cash register was, even knowing where the security camera was in the shops that had one, deciding what would fit under his hoodie or in the pockets of his baggy jeans.

Waiting for the man at the counter to turn his head. Jayson smiling his fake smile, even waving on his way out the door. Hating himself for what he was doing. But telling himself, every single time, that he did what he needed to survive.

Now he walked up the aisle with cookies and a drink in his hand, thinking about how good it felt that he didn't have to do that anymore.

As he made his way to the cash register, feeling like luck was finally on his side, he spotted Mrs. Montgomery—Zoe's mom—leaning on her shopping cart, talking to a woman Jayson didn't recognize.

It was almost like thinking about his luck had made it run out right there and then.

He didn't want her to see him, didn't want to talk to her. The one time he'd been in her house he'd gotten the feeling that she didn't like him being there, felt like she'd looked down on him, even though when he'd mentioned that to Zoe later she said he was being crazy, that her mom was just surprised to see him.

Mrs. Montgomery pushed her cart forward to make room for another woman with a cart. Jayson was reaching for some

Doritos, planning to get out of the store before she saw him.

Then he heard his name.

"Have I told you about her new friend, this Jayson boy?" Mrs. Montgomery said.

She wasn't speaking loudly. But he was only about ten feet away, hidden from her by some kind of display.

"The new boy?"

"The one Tom and Carol took in."

"It was so generous of them."

"I suppose." Mrs. Montgomery dragged out the last word, as if she didn't think it was so generous. "But that boy comes from dirt."

"What, because he comes from the other side of town?" her friend said.

"Oh, that's the least of it," Mrs. Montgomery said. "I heard he's a *thief*."

Jayson was frozen in place, afraid to even breathe. A brand new kind of being afraid.

"One of Kevin's friends teaches at Moreland East Middle," she continued. "And he mentioned to Kevin one day that their best basketball player had ended up at Belmont. *This* boy, Jayson. And Kevin said he knew him, that he'd been to our house and was friends with Zoe."

Kevin had to be Zoe's dad.

"Anyway," Zoe's mom continued, "he proceeded to tell Kevin that the boy's story was like some modern-day Dickens tale. Nobody at the school had been aware that a twelve-year-old boy had been living on his own after his mother died, until he got caught stealing a pair of sneakers over in Percy. That was how he ended up in Child Protective Services."

"Unbelievable."

Jayson was afraid to even breathe. Afraid, period. The thing he'd feared most was happening right here and right now. His new world finding out secrets about his old one.

"It makes sense, really." Zoe's mom sounded like she was enjoying every minute of her story. "The mother was dirt as well."

"What do you mean?" her friend asked.

"Well, she died recently. Drugs, apparently. Figures. You know where they were living, right? The *Pines*." Mrs. Montgomery sighed and said, "God only knows what his role in the whole mess was."

"What are you saying?"

"Well, I can't be certain, of course, but maybe the boy was dealing drugs himself. How else did the family manage to get by? No father figure, a drug-addicted mother, in that environment. Connect the dots."

Zoe's mom thought he was a criminal, a drug dealer. She *knew* about his stealing. And then piled on a made-up crime.

All those times that he had pictured Zoe or his teammates finding out the truth, finding out that he had stolen just to get by, he thought he could at least get them to understand what it'd been like living on his own. But how could he explain away things that hadn't even happened? Jayson wanted to run away, hide. But he was frozen in place.

The next thing he heard: "Well, once I found out, I had to tell Zoe. Just so she knew the whole story about her new friend. I didn't tell her to stop seeing him, that's the wrong approach to take with my daughter, believe me. I'm not looking to hurt the boy. But I certainly don't have to have him in my house. I mean, really."

Was that why Zoe hadn't been around much lately?

Did it matter? He knew this: Enough of what Zoe had been told was true, no getting around it.

Jayson thought about his visit to the Montgomerys' house, the way Zoe had suddenly changed the way she acted once her mother came around. Maybe it was another part of being Miss Perfect, even though she'd said she hated being treated that way. Maybe Zoe felt trapped in her box just like Jayson did his.

"So do they still see each other away from school?" the friend asked.

"As little as possible," Mrs. Montgomery said, "though Kevin is bringing Zoe into town so she can have lunch with the boy today."

The boy thought: *Not anymore.*

Suddenly, he had someplace he needed to be.

AS JAYSON LOOKED AROUND, HE thought, somehow, despite everything that had changed in his life, some things would always stay the same.

The buildings around him looked exactly the same. Buildings that had probably looked old even when they had been brand new. The playground at the far end, closest to the building, was empty in the late afternoon, maybe because the day had gotten a lot colder in the last couple of hours, especially once the sun had gone down. This part of North Carolina didn't feel like winter all that often, but it did today.

Maybe that's why nobody was playing ball on the court at the Jeff.

It had never been too cold or too dark for Jayson when he'd played here. But no matter what, no matter how late he'd been out there by himself, he'd never felt afraid. Or lost. Not as long as he had a ball in his hands. Jayson had always known exactly who he was on a basketball court.

Not the person he'd just heard Mrs. Montgomery describe to her friend. The *real* person he knew he was.

For once in his life, though, he hadn't come here to play.

Maybe Tyrese or Shabazz would look out a window, spot him, come down and want to know why he'd come back without telling anybody.

Why had he come?

He'd come here with Zoe Montgomery on his mind. What she now knew about him. And what he knew about her. It was all somehow cloudy, like he was trying to make out an image through fog.

Truth and lies.

All this time he had worried about her finding out he'd stolen the shoes. Or that he'd stolen when he didn't have the money to buy food. But those things seemed like nothing now.

She knew that the reason he had ended up at her school, and in her life, was because he had stolen those shoes. But she and her mom must've thought that was nothing compared to the drugs. He'd made mistakes in his life, but never anything like drugs. He'd sworn to himself long ago, after watching his mother during one of her "sick" periods, that he would never *ever* touch the rotten things. And how could anyone even *think* that he would have supplied her with that stuff? Drugs stole his mother from him long before Jayson had stolen a thing. He hated even thinking about it.

That wasn't who he was . . .

Was it? Did stealing to get by mean that he was a bad person?

His mom had told him, at the end, that she didn't have the

strength to protect him any longer. Now Zoe's mom was doing what she thought she had to do to protect Zoe.

Protecting her from me, he thought. He understood wanting to protect someone.

He'd always known, deep down, that his mom was sad, that she was fighting a monster bigger and stronger than she was. Yet she was still his mother and he'd loved her. He remembered wishing he could fight that monster for her, somehow take the sadness out of her and make it disappear.

He hadn't been strong enough back then. Hadn't known what to do, or how.

He checked the time on his phone and wondered if Mrs. Lawton was starting to worry about him, even though it had only been a couple of hours since she'd dropped him off in town. He'd texted her when he'd gotten on the bus to the east side to say that he was going to hang out with some old friends for a while.

Sort of true. This court was his oldest friend in a lot of ways. It never let him down.

On the other side of the playground, he heard the sound of a couple of small kids laughing as they walked ahead of their mom, who was carrying two grocery bags, all of them on their way into the Jeff.

Jayson smiled. Not at the kids, but at a memory. He was remembering when he was their age, when all he worried about was his next game on the court.

This place, it was a part of him.

But it wasn't all of him. He never would've thought it would happen, but he'd grown to like parts of his new life. Liked the stability of the Lawtons, and his new teammates were good guys.

Jayson knew he would always be a kid from East Moreland. Would always be the kid who had stolen to get by, just like he was the kid who never wanted to leave the basketball court. Even he wasn't fast enough to escape his own past or where he was from.

But that didn't make him the person Mrs. Montgomery claimed he was. He might never be able to change that part, either.

Maybe that was no big deal.

Maybe all that mattered was that he knew the truth about himself.

Maybe he always had.

29

JAYSON SENT A TEXT TO Mrs. Lawton when he transferred to the bus that would take him back to town, and she picked him up at the Village Market.

He'd come full circle.

He had already decided not to tell her what he had heard inside the market from Mrs. Montgomery. And he definitely didn't plan to tell Zoe, either.

He had just one thought now, one goal. Move forward. Get himself where he wanted to be: Cameron Indoor Stadium, playing for the North Carolina middle school championship.

When he got into the car, Mrs. Lawton said, "What in the world have you been doing all this time?"

"It was kind of a spur-of-the-moment thing," he said, "but I decided to go over and hang out at the Jeff for a while."

"Really," she said.

"Totally unplanned. Hope you don't mind I didn't tell you I was going."

"Depends. How did it go?"

"It actually went great."

"Are you being sarcastic?"

He shook his head. "Nope. Being honest. I just needed to see it again. Remember where I came from."

"Where *we* came from."

Jayson smiled at that.

When they pulled into the driveway, Mrs. Lawton said that dinner would be ready in about fifteen minutes. Jayson went upstairs, took out his phone, and saw that he had two missed calls from Zoe, to go with all the texts he'd started getting from her about ten minutes after he was supposed to show up at the diner.

He knew he was going to have to respond, even if he didn't know what to say. He remembered the fear he'd felt listening to Zoe's mom in the supermarket and thought about not facing Zoe again until school on Monday, but he knew that putting off his explanation would only make things worse.

So he texted her now.

So sorry. Phone died. Had to do something really important.

It didn't take long for her to hit him back.

That's it? I waited for you for an hour.

I'm sorry. I know I messed up...

U messed up? That's your excuse?

Something came up. Don't know what else to say.

He knew he had come up with a lame excuse. But he *was* sorry. He just didn't see the point in telling her the whole big story right then. Even if he knew the truth about himself, that didn't mean that Zoe would believe it.

Yet he wanted her to. Eventually.

Call you later?

She wasn't having it.

Maybe MY phone will die.

He knew he deserved that. And would wear it.

After dinner was over, Jayson went upstairs to check the NBA scores on his computer. Still thinking about what had happened at the Village Market, he couldn't get up the nerve to call Zoe. And she didn't call him.

He didn't call or text her on Sunday, either. They didn't get a chance to talk until they were coming out of English together on Monday morning.

"I thought you were going to call," she said.

"I got the feeling you were still mad at me."

"Well, you were right," she said. "But you still should have called."

"Sorry." It was getting to be a habit, using that word.

They walked in silence down the hall until she said, "So?"

"So what?"

"Are you going to tell me what was so important that you left me hanging without saying anything?"

"It's a long, boring story," he said.

"I've got time."

"Something happened that afternoon. But I'd really rather not talk about it."

They arrived at their lockers. Zoe remained silent.

"I said I'm sorry and I meant it. Are you gonna accept my apology?" Jayson asked.

"You're really not going to tell me?"

Jayson wanted to. But the words just wouldn't come.

"Fine, then," Zoe said. "Be that way."

As she walked away, another boy from their English class joined her. Jayson recognized him right away. Eric Kelly, the kid he'd seen practicing his moves at Zoe's soccer game. Jayson couldn't hear what he said to her, but whatever it was, it made her laugh.

Friday afternoon, after practice had ended, Bryan walked up to Jayson, big smile on his face. "Do you ever get tired of being in the gym? Sometimes I'm convinced that you sleep here."

Jayson grinned back at him. "What do you mean sometimes?"

"It does seem to be working for you."

"The harder I work, the better I get," Jayson said. "And the harder *we* work the better *we* get."

Practice had ended a half hour ago, but the Bobcats were just getting ready to leave the court now because they'd decided to stay and scrimmage among themselves, working on a few new plays Coach had come up with. The next day they were playing the Percy Central Hawks away.

They were all sitting on the floor in front of their bench. Cameron had a towel over his head, sucking down some water. Brandon was doing the same. Cameron picked his head up and said to Jayson, "You've been even more crazed on the court than ever this week, you know that, right?"

Jayson shrugged. "Now that the end of the season is getting closer, I want it even more."

"We all want it," Brandon said. "We're talking Coach K's house. It doesn't get much bigger than Cameron Indoor."

"Or much better."

Bryan drank the last of the red Gatorade in his bottle. "You believe we're good enough to go all the way?"

Jayson looked at him. "Where else would we be going?"

He had decided that was the only way his story could end, at least for now. He kept telling himself there had to be a reason that he had ended up in this particular gym, playing with this team. He would never say that everything he'd gone through to get here was worth it. Or that it had been easy on him, because it hadn't. But he knew it had made him stronger. And he believed it had made him a better basketball player.

He knew so many of the stories about the greatest players in basketball. He'd heard that amazing speech Kevin Durant had given after he'd won his first MVP Award in 2014, talking about how his mom had been the real MVP in his life, all the jobs she'd held and all the sacrifices she'd made to give him his chance.

Maybe Debbie Barnes could have been that kind of mom if life hadn't crushed her the way it had. Or if she had just been a little stronger herself, if she'd been as strong as Jayson had become.

But no matter what, she'd helped him to become the person he was today. Mrs. Montgomery could say what she wanted, but that didn't change the fact that Jayson's mom had tried her best.

The NBA was filled with players whose mothers had done their best. He knew about how difficult LeBron's life had been growing up in Akron, Ohio, until basketball had been his ticket out.

Jayson was more determined than ever that basketball would be his ticket out, too.

30

JAYSON WASN'T ALL THAT EXCITED about going back to Percy; it brought back all the memories of the worst and dumbest day of his life, the way those memories had come flooding back the day Pete from Foot Locker had walked into the pizza place.

But he kept telling himself that once the game started at Percy, basketball would be the only thing on his mind. Somehow, Percy was the only team to have beaten Moreland East during the regular season. Twice. And the Bobcats had already lost once to Percy, by one point, at home, earlier in the season. Their only other loss of the season aside from their first game against Moreland East.

The Percy Hawks, in their cool black jerseys and pants, had overtaken the Mavericks to grab first place. So everybody in the gym knew how big this game was. But then, every game they would play the rest of the way was big, all of the teams bunched near the top trying to hold their positions, three teams for two spots in the title game. The Bobcats and Mavericks were both 9–2, and Percy was 10–1, which meant all three teams still had a good shot at making it to the league championship game.

But there was still a ways to go before that happened.

Whoever did end up winning the league championship game would earn a spot in the county tournament to play against the winners of three other leagues. And if you won that, you went to the big tournament at Cameron Indoor, a competition among the top eight middle-grade teams in the state.

Jayson noticed Bryan and Cameron staring at him a couple of minutes before they were supposed to take the court.

"What?" he said.

Cameron grinned. "Oh, nothing."

"What are you two staring at?"

Bryan grinned now, and pointed at Jayson's legs. When Jayson looked down, he saw them bouncing up and down.

Cameron said, "I was worried that we might be having some kind of earthquake, the way the floor was shaking. Then I realized it was just you."

"Very funny," Jayson said.

"My mom's always talking about *my* nervous energy; that's what she calls it," Cameron said. "But there has to be a whole other word for what you've got going."

"I'm not nervous," Jayson said. "Just ready. Question is: are you?"

Cameron nodded. "We got this."

Coach Rooney, who'd been out in the hall visiting with the

Percy coach, opened the locker room door. "Okay, boys, let's get this party started."

The Percy Hawks weren't particularly big. Cameron and Brandon were the tallest guys on the court. But the Hawks had a nice motion offense, passing the ball around constantly, not forcing any shots, finding open looks, so by the time the first quarter was over, Jayson was pretty sure everybody in their starting lineup had scored at least one basket.

Even though they didn't have the height to match up with the Belmont big men, Percy was still ahead by ten points, and had outplayed the Bobcats on both ends of the court. The Bobcats had been struggling to keep up with Percy's fast-paced play, so Jayson thought the score could have been worse than it was.

Cameron and Brandon hadn't been able to capitalize on their mismatches, but the fact that the Bobcats were being beaten was hardly their fault. Jayson was being outplayed badly by Percy's point guard, JeMarcus Betts, who'd been hurt the first time the two teams had played. And Percy had *still* won that game. Jayson had only heard about how good JeMarcus was. Today he was seeing it with his own eyes.

He was the same size as Jayson and just as quick. Maybe even quicker, though Jayson hated admitting that to himself. JeMarcus was staying in front of Jayson on defense, barely giving him an inch to work with, then blowing past him on offense, finding open lanes while Jayson was hitting nothing but dead ends. Jayson was getting lit up, no point denying it. JeMarcus was throwing him off his game totally, frustrating him all over the court.

"I can't believe I'm letting this guy beat me!" Jayson said to Bryan in the middle of the second quarter, the Hawks up fourteen by then.

They were standing at midcourt while the Hawks' small forward shot free throws, Jayson trying to keep his voice low even though he was spitting mad. He'd already been benched once for talking back.

"Still a lot of game to play," Bryan said. "Time to get your head *back* in it."

Jayson jerked his head in Bryan's direction, started to say something. But then he stopped himself.

Because he knew Bryan was right. He was beating himself now just as much as JeMarcus was. Maybe more.

But nothing changed. The harder Jayson tried, the worse things seemed to get. He told himself to stop forcing passes and shots . . . and then kept forcing passes and shots. With about two minutes left in the half, Jayson tried to make a play on defense after JeMarcus flew by him again, swiping at the ball as JeMarcus went past him.

The whistle blew, the ref pointing at Jayson.

"All ball!" he yelled at the ref. "Are you blind?"

He knew he was in trouble right away, knew he should have kept his mouth shut. Knew it didn't matter if it had really been a foul or not. But it was too late.

The ref glared at Jayson, slammed his right palm down on the extended fingers of his left hand, T'ing Jayson up.

Not only would JeMarcus shoot the one-and-one for the foul

Jayson had just committed, but he'd also get two more free throws for the technical foul. And then the Hawks would get the ball back. It could turn into a six-point play for the Hawks, at a time when the Bobcats couldn't afford to fall farther behind.

"And, son?" the ref said. "Not another word out of you the rest of the game, or you're gone. Am I making myself clear?"

Jayson nodded.

"I didn't quite catch that."

"Yes, sir," Jayson said. Then he shut his big mouth.

Coach Rooney already had Alex Ahmad up, waiting by the scorer's table to enter the game. Coach motioned for Jayson to come sit next to him. But he didn't say anything then, or for the rest of the half, which Jayson watched in silence, wondering what kind of look was on his coach's face now but not daring to find out.

Coach didn't call Jayson out in the locker room at halftime, or show him up in front of his teammates. He just stood calmly in the middle of the room and told them what he'd observed on the court, how they needed to change things up on offense by not crowding the lane and using back screens more often, and how they all had to do a better job of moving their feet on defense, fighting harder through screens, getting better position under the boards.

"We're down only fourteen, and since I know what brilliant students of basketball you all are, I don't have to tell you that we're lucky it's only fourteen," Coach said. "But we can't rely on luck in the second half; only skill is going to give us a shot.

And you know what? We have a lot of talent on this team, so by the time the third quarter is over, this is going to be a game. And by the end, I believe it's going to be a game we win."

They all nodded.

"As far as I know, no coach has ever drawn up a fourteen-point play," he said. "Let's do this one possession at a time. You with me?"

Heads nodded all over the locker room.

"I can't hear you."

"Yes, Coach!" every voice shouted at once.

"That's more like it."

Jayson waited until the other players were out of the locker room, but he didn't wait for Coach to approach him, knowing the right thing to do was to own up to his mistake.

"I'm sorry about yelling like that. Just got so frustrated out there."

Coach sat down next to him on the bench. "What's going on?"

"I stink, that's what's going on."

"If you were more tightly wound," Coach said, "I think I could fit you inside one of my golf balls."

"We need this game!"

"Nah," Coach said. "We want it real bad. But we don't need it. The world won't end if we lose this game."

"I can't believe you're saying that," Jayson said. "We've got a great chance to finish *first* in this league. Nobody thought at the beginning of the season, not even me, that we could finish on top. We have a shot to beat out the Hawks and Mavericks and get home court for the championship game."

Jayson realized he was breathing hard.

"Did something happen to you that I should know about?" Coach said. "For once, it feels like there's more than basketball at stake with you."

For a split second, Jayson thought about telling him about the whole situation with Zoe and her mom, but then he remembered his promise to himself to keep it to himself. He had enough problems on the court today, no need to make more.

"No," he said.

"Jayson, I know how much you've taken on. New school, new team, new family. But don't make this all bigger than it is. Like I said, take it one play at a time. One game at a time."

He put a hand on Jayson's shoulder.

"You're better than their point guard. You're letting him get to you, which is what he wants. You need to play your game out there. They can't beat us if you do that. Only way we lose is if you do the job for them and beat yourself."

By the time they got back on the court, the big scoreboard was counting down the last minute of halftime. Coach Rooney had just enough time to tell the rest of the Bobcats that he was going with the same five that had started the game.

But you wouldn't have known it was the same guys by watching them play—it was almost like Coach's talk had transformed them, like a whole different group of players had walked out onto the court. Cameron and Brandon were making use of their height advantages now, posting up left and right, making their size difference count, getting one rebound after another. And Jayson? He'd cooled down some, though he was always at least a little heated when a game was going on. But now he was seeing the court more clearly. Hounding JeMarcus on defense, barely catching his breath before launching into another fast break, sometimes taking it all the way himself, other times dishing it to his teammates.

Halfway through the third quarter, the Bobcats had cut the Hawks' lead almost in half, to 36–27. In the last few plays, Jayson had gotten a couple of quick assists, one to Rashard, one to Bryan. Trying to get everyone involved like the Hawks had done in the first half.

Next Bobcats' possession, Jayson worked a sweet give-and-go with Brandon, breaking loose on his cut for an easy layup, beating JeMarcus.

36–29, Percy.

At the other end of the court, he had just one goal: stop JeMarcus from getting around him at all costs. Jayson didn't mind letting him go from side to side—"east-west defense," as Coach called it—but if he wanted to push himself and the ball toward the basket, Jayson was determined to make him work for every inch.

Mostly he was trying to follow Coach's advice, taking it one play at a time. Just telling himself that if he could win his battle with the kid the Hawks called JBetts, maybe the Bobcats really could come all the way back.

Jayson wasn't shutting JeMarcus down completely; the guy was too good for that. But at least Jayson had slowed him down and made him show a little frustration of his own.

Coach gave Jayson a two-minute rest to start the fourth quarter. Though he'd had trouble throughout the season with the ball in his hands, Alex Ahmad was strong defensively, and he did a good job on JeMarcus while out there, giving up just one basket when he got lost on a switch, but making up for it on the other end when he sank a crazy three-pointer off the glass as the shot clock expired.

Hawks up by six when Jayson came back in the game.

Cameron came over and said, "They're the ones who are tight now. They're playing like they're afraid to lose."

"Then let's see if we can scare the life out of them the rest of the way."

"Sounds like a plan."

Little by little, the Percy lead got smaller, the Bobcats looking like they'd saved their best basketball for the end of the game, when it counted the most.

Cameron and Jayson were doing what they'd done all season, tag-teaming Percy, blocking shots, stealing passes, give-and-gos for days. The Bobcats had put their weak first-half performance in the rearview, never looking back.

With thirty-two seconds left and the Hawks up by only two, Jayson used a crossover dribble to get past JeMarcus. JeMarcus saw it happening and reached out with a desperate swipe at the ball, getting Jayson's arm instead. Jayson continued his motion through the foul and made the layup that tied the game. The last of Percy's big lead was gone.

Jayson sank the free throw to give the Bobcats their first lead of the day.

The Percy coach called time-out. As the 'Cats came over to their bench, Jayson looked up into the stands to where the Lawtons were standing with the rest of the Belmont parents, Bryan's parents on one side of them, Cameron's on the other.

Mrs. Lawton made a motion like she was trying to raise the roof with both hands above her head. He looked at her, shaking his head sadly, and saw her laugh.

Coach said, "Boys, there's *still* a lot of basketball to be played. Let's get a stop right here. We've worked too hard and played too well to let these boys think this game is theirs if they want it back. They've been working their butts off trying to get past our defense, so keep up the pressure. And when we do get a stop, I want you all to be ready to bust it down the court. But don't force anything. Play our game and we'll be taking a win all the way back to Belmont."

As Jayson started to leave the huddle, Coach put a hand on his arm.

"They're going to clear out for Betts," Coach Rooney said. "He's still their best player. The ball has to be in his hands at the end."

Jayson looked at his coach and said, "Can't wait."

Jayson knew Coach was right. The Hawks had to take their chances with JeMarcus. Give *him* a chance to win the game.

And that's exactly what happened. The Hawks cleared out for JBetts. Point guard vs. point guard. JeMarcus didn't have the size to back Jayson in for a post-up shot over the top. So he did what he did best, using his speed and ball skills, coming at Jayson head-on, making Jayson move his feet to try and stay in front. Jayson focused on the center of his man's chest the way he'd always been taught, not watching JeMarcus's eyes or the ball, not wanting to bite on a head fake or a ball fake.

Jayson had been covering this guy almost all game, studying all his moves. He prided himself on paying close attention to his opponents. Looking for any weaknesses he could exploit. One time he'd stopped to watch poker on ESPN and heard one of the announcers talking about how some players had "tells," a way of unintentionally hinting to the other players at the table what they were going to do.

JBetts had one: When he wanted to drive right, he had a tendency to keep his eyes focused toward his left while taking one left-handed dribble, trying to get Jayson to lean that way just a little before going hard right.

It was the move he tried on Jayson now.

Jayson was ready for it.

He didn't flinch, didn't put himself in a position where he would have to react and maybe get whistled for a cheap foul. Instead, he just slid to the right to cut JeMarcus off, timing the motion perfectly as the Percy point guard stepped out in the same direction.

It startled JeMarcus just enough, blew up the move he was trying to pull off, and caused him to look up at Jayson for just an instant. All it takes sometimes. Jayson flicked out his hand and stole the ball mid-dribble. He had a step on JeMarcus and that was plenty. Jayson raced the length of the court on the fast break and kissed the ball off the glass for a layup.

Bobcats by three with just eighteen seconds left.

One more stop—that was all they needed. They could even give up an easy two just to run time off the clock and take possession again.

But Jayson had a hunch the Hawks wouldn't take the chance of giving the 'Cats the ball back. They would go for the tie, a three-pointer. And there was only one player on the Hawks who was a good enough shot to take it.

JeMarcus.

Just before the Hawks inbounded the ball, Jayson whispered something into Cameron's ear.

The Bobcats let the Hawks inbound to JeMarcus and gave him the floor. Jayson waited for him just past midcourt, knees bent, on the balls of his feet. Ready to react, but letting the game come to him. Cameron stood at the top of the paint, loosely guarding the Percy center.

JeMarcus crossed midcourt. As soon as he did, Cameron left his man and raced to Jayson's left. Jayson shifted to the right and planted his feet. JeMarcus was caught in the trap. Jayson wasn't about to let him get past, and the double-team from Cameron took away every other option except for a blind pass, and Jayson knew that JeMarcus wasn't about to give up the rock. Even with the Hawks' center standing wide open beneath the basket, calling for the ball.

Frustrated, JeMarcus plowed right over Jayson, who hit the ground, knowing as he did so that the whistle he heard would be for a charging foul against JeMarcus. All Jayson needed to do was sink one foul shot and the game would be over.

Which he did.

After the clock ran out and the Bobcats celebrated, Coach approached Jayson. "That double-team. Your call?"

Jayson nodded. "Just taking it one play at a time" He smiled and said, "I'm very well coached that way."

THERE WAS A PART OF him that kept expecting something else to go wrong, just because so many things had gone wrong for him in his life.

The memory of overhearing Zoe's mom tell terrible lies about him was still fresh in his mind.

Yet he'd proven to himself that he could get through the worst life had to throw his way. Jayson knew already, at twelve, living one life when the school year started and another one now, how much fight he had in him. How he never stayed down for long.

He still felt mad sometimes, and probably always would, to the point where it took everything he had to calm himself. But he knew he was getting better at it. Day by day and game by game. Ms. Moretti had taught him to imagine a bubble filled with his anger when he started feeling that way.

"A bubble?"

"Yes, sir."

"And what do I do with the bubble?"

She smiled, spread out her arms wide. "Pop that sucker!"

"Instead of letting myself pop, you mean?"

"Couldn't have said it better myself."

He tried using Ms. Moretti's technique when things weren't going his way on the court. Lately, though, he hadn't needed to use it too often. There had been times when he'd thought the Bobcats couldn't be as good as they were playing. But the wins had kept on coming.

Now there were just two games left in the regular season, and if they won those last two games, they would play in the league championship game.

Nearly everything in his life seemed to be going right. Everything except his friendship with Zoe. No matter how many times he told himself that things between them could never be the way they used to be, that they were hiding too many secrets from each other, he still wanted them to be friends.

Maybe it was because he'd never had a girl in his life before. Or maybe it was just this girl in particular. But no matter how many times he tried to find the words to tell her the truth, he'd always shut down when the time came to actually speak up. He wanted to explain to her that he wasn't really a thief, that he'd just made a mistake, that what he'd done, taking those sneakers, wasn't really him. More importantly, he wanted to separate the truth from the lies, make her understand that he'd never had his hands on drugs, even somebody else's, once in his whole life. For some reason, though, he couldn't find the courage to come out and say that.

Oh, he and Zoe kept going through the motions of still

being friends. It wasn't as if they were avoiding each other altogether. They just never hung out after school anymore. Never had any real conversations.

Jayson still wasn't ready to give up.

The Friday afternoon before the game against the Geffen Grizzlies, Jayson tried to talk out the problem with Ms. Moretti. Yet when she tried to get him to reveal some details, Jayson shut down again.

"Even when you're putting yourself out there," she said, "you still hold back." She shook her head. "Man, it must be tough staying so tough."

"Some things you have to keep to yourself."

"Fair. So without giving away the full story, what's really bothering you?"

"That I should've been honest from the beginning, and now I've made a mistake I can't undo."

They were in the Lawtons' living room, as usual. She just let his words hang there in the air for the moment.

"People make mistakes, Jayson," Ms. Moretti said in a soft voice. "But sometimes, owning up to them can make things right."

"Not if those mistakes take on a life of their own. It's too late now."

"You can't know that. All you can do is guess and remain afraid of finding out. How will you ever know if you don't give it a shot? Seems to me the ball's in your hands."

She had a point. He had nothing to lose by trying—nothing else seemed to be working with Zoe Montgomery these days.

32

FIRST THERE WAS THE BUSINESS of the game against Geffen. The Grizzlies had lost both of their starting guards halfway through the season and had only two wins, but too much was at stake for the Bobcats to be looking ahead. They needed this one to keep their championship hopes alive. Win this game and get to next Saturday, where Jayson would not only have a chance to help his team make it to the title game, he would also get another opportunity to beat his old team.

Throughout most of the game against the Grizzlies, Jayson had no reason to think that next week's game against Moreland East wouldn't be the one he was hoping for, with everything on the line. The 'Cats were at the top of their game against Geffen, building up an eleven-point lead by halftime and at one point stretching it to seventeen in the third quarter. Jayson barely even noticed as the Grizzlies started to chip away at the lead.

With four minutes to go, the 'Cats still held a thirteen-point lead. Jayson couldn't help it—he began thinking about that next game against Moreland East and all it would mean.

Huge mistake.

While in the beginning of the game it seemed the Bobcats could do no wrong, suddenly they weren't doing *anything* right. It was like the whole team had decided to break down all at once, like they were *all* looking ahead to the rematch with Moreland East. It started with a couple of quick baskets for Geffen on plays that the Bobcats had been stopping all game long. It grew worse when Brandon fouled out, committing a dumb one far away from the basket. That meant Cameron, who had just committed his fourth foul, didn't even have time to catch his breath on the bench. Coach had no choice—he had to get Cameron back in.

But Cameron actually needed that time on the bench. He was tired, and it showed. Finding himself out of position on his first possession back in, he reached over the top of the Grizzlies' center and now he, too, had fouled out.

Two free throws for the Grizzlies. They made them both.

Six quick points for Geffen.

Bobcats by only seven now.

Then Jayson, frustrated at what he saw slipping away, tried to force a pass to Bryan that ended up in the hands of a Geffen player, who ran it down the court. Jayson, mad at himself, lagged behind defensively, giving the Grizzlies a momentary advantage. Bryan's man kicked the ball out to Jayson's man, who was all alone at the top of the key, the fifth player in a five-on-four fast break. Three-pointer, nothing but net.

Just like that, the lead was down to four. A 9–0 run for

Geffen. The flow of the game could change in a heartbeat in sports, one team taking momentum away from the other. It was exactly what the Geffen Grizzlies were doing to the Belmont Bobcats. Both teams knew.

Right after the three-pointer, Bryan came up short on a wide-open look, which led to a fast break for the Grizzlies, and an easy layup.

With a minute left, the lead was two points. What had looked like an easy win now had a chance to be their worst loss of the season. Jayson brought the ball down and passed it off to Bryan, showing confidence in his shooting guard even though he'd been missing in the last few minutes. Bryan missed again, but got fouled shooting the jumper. When he got to the line, he had a chance to stretch the lead back to four, give Belmont some breathing room. Bryan had been an 80-percent foul shooter throughout the season, easily the best on the team.

He missed them both, barely touching the front of the rim with the second one.

Every player on the Bobcats was playing tight now, their confidence completely gone, the way their lead was.

Then Deion Daniels, the Grizzlies' best player, had the ball in his hands again, with a chance to tie, or even take the lead with a three.

No way, Jayson thought. This time he was the first one back on defense, running hard as soon as the Geffen center had come down with the rebound. But Bryan was slow getting back on his man, a converted forward named Kenny Wright. Kenny only had a step on him. But in basketball, that was all it took. Deion hit him with a perfect bounce pass, Jayson having no shot at batting it away, so Kenny took the ball, and then he kissed it against the glass for a score.

Game tied. The Bobcats in a total freefall now. The only question was when they would hit bottom.

Coach stood up, called time, and waved them over.

As they headed toward the bench, Bryan came up alongside Jayson and said, "I'm scared I'm going to do something to lose us this game."

"Then go tell Coach to take you out," Jayson said.

Maybe Bryan was expecting a pep talk from Jayson in that moment. Or words of encouragement. He certainly didn't expect to hear what he'd just heard.

He reacted as if Jayson had slapped him. "What did you just say?"

"Tell him to take you out. You're scared about a basketball game? Then maybe you don't belong in one."

They needed this game. And he knew Bryan couldn't play it scared. He was just trying to give his teammate some steel, get him mad and ready to take it out on the Grizzlies.

Coach kept it simple. He always did, whether it was the first quarter of the game or the last minute of the fourth. His voice was upbeat, acting like this was the only place he wanted to be, wanting his team to feel the same way.

The opposite of scared. Full of steel himself.

He grinned and said, "I've got nothing." Trying to lighten the mood.

Jayson heard some nervous laughter behind him.

"What I *mean* is," Coach Rooney said, "I don't think we should run a set play. By now they know everything in our playbook. The ball's in your hands on this one, Jayson. The rest of you, spread the court while Jayson gets the offense in motion. Keep on passing like we've been doing so well all season, use up the clock, and then when we get our chance—and I know we will—don't be afraid to take the shot that wins us the game. How does that sound?"

Jayson answered for all of them. "Love it."

"You know they'll put Deion on you for the last play," Coach said. "If he tries to be a hero and go for a steal, make him pay."

Jayson nodded.

"This is our game to lose," Coach said. "But we're not going to do that, are we?"

"Not a chance," Jayson said.

Jayson refused to accept the possibility that they were going to lose this game after having dominated for so much of it. But he knew they had to win the game right here and now, because they weren't beating the Grizzlies in overtime without Cameron or Brandon.

Twenty-four seconds left when they inbounded the ball. Enough time for one play if Belmont milked it, with the shot clock turned off.

The Bobcats spread the court like Coach had told them to do. Bryan ran to the left corner, his sweet spot. Jayson threw him the ball. But Bryan was well defended, the Geffen defense on high alert, not giving up any easy looks, so Bryan gave it back to Jayson, running to the other corner as Marty Samuels left that spot and got himself open to give Jayson an out. Jayson handed the ball off to Marty, who got jammed up a second later, and gave it right back to Jayson.

Jayson thought they were passing the ball around like they were playing a game of hot potato.

Fifteen seconds.

Jayson felt his heart pounding. Good nerves, he knew. He hated losing, but he never played afraid. He was just like Coach in this moment: right where he wanted to be.

He dribbled back to the top of the circle. Deion stayed with him. He saw Deion look past him, probably checking the clock at the other end. Time was running out fast.

It turned out Deion wasn't interested in letting the game go to overtime either. Just like Jayson, he wanted to win in regulation.

So Deion went for the steal.

Just a quick lunge, hand out, careful not to foul. But Jayson had been watching Deion's hands, waiting for him to make his move, dribbling being like breathing for Jayson, who didn't need to keep his eyes on the ball. So Jayson wasn't just ready for him, he was already on his way past him.

Nine seconds left.

There was an open lane to the basket. But it closed up fast, the Grizzlies' center cutting Jayson off. It was one of those moments when Jayson felt as if he could see the whole court, like a quarterback with all day to throw, scanning the field, everyone in motion now. He saw Bryan's man, Kenny, coming over to cover Kyle, filling in at center for Belmont now that Cameron and Brandon were out, leaving Bryan open on the right side.

Jammed up in the lane by the Grizzlies' center, Jayson used his left hand to shoot a cool behind-the-back pass to Bryan, who caught the ball, squared up his shoulders, and let it fly.

The ball looked a little short. But Bryan had shot it softly enough, put just enough air underneath it, that it touched the front of the rim, then the back of the rim, and finally fell through the net for the basket that won them the game.

Bryan looked more surprised than anybody. Maybe he understood that he had defeated more than the Geffen Grizzlies in that moment.

Jayson ran over to him and the two jumped at each other in the air.

When they came down, Jayson said, "Now what are you afraid of?"

Bryan laughed, then shouted at Jayson, "You!"

THE WEEK LEADING UP TO the game at Moreland East to decide which team would make it to the league championship was a blur to Jayson Barnes.

Jayson went to his classes, he went through his normal routine when he'd see Zoe, both of them pretending that nothing had changed between them. He still planned to talk to her. Just not right now.

He wasn't letting anything get in the way of basketball, not this week.

He'd do his homework at night, but ten minutes after he'd finish, he couldn't remember a thing he'd read, or written. It was the same with the basketball games he watched on television after he was done studying. He'd know which teams won, he just couldn't remember how in the world they did it.

He kept thinking of being back in his old school, going up against Ty and Shabazz one more time.

As the season went on, he'd spent less and less time talking to Ty, to the point where right now they were hardly communicating at all. Finally, last night, Ty had broken the silence and called him.

"Hey, Snap. Are we still good?" he said.

Snap. It was a name Jayson barely heard these days. Like it had disappeared.

"Always," Jayson said. "I'm just focused on winning right now. We'll be better when the game is over."

"After we stomp you out, you mean?"

Jayson felt himself grinning. "Lot's changed this year, Ty. But you still talk the same old trash."

"I talk it 'cause I can walk it."

"We're gonna find out soon enough."

The only place where things made sense to Jayson—shocker—was in the gym. But he couldn't spend all day in the gym, much less sleep there, so the Friday night before the game, Jayson was sitting in the kitchen with the Lawtons, eating dinner.

Didn't mean he wasn't talking about the game, though.

"I know I'm probably making this game bigger in my own mind than it really is," he said to the Lawtons.

"Gee," Mrs. Lawton said, "I hadn't picked up on that. Had *you* picked up on it, Tom?"

Mr. Lawton shook his head. "Nope. Not me. Business as usual around here, far as I could tell."

Jayson said, "I didn't know when I moved in here how funny you two are."

"Oh, we were *always* funny," Mr. Lawton said. "You're just late to the party."

"Seriously, though," Mrs. Lawton said, "only one more day

until game day, and then you can put this out of your mind."

"I can't believe it's finally here," Jayson said. "It feels like I've been waiting forever to get another shot at them, just because of the way I cost us the first game."

"Wasn't just you, as I recall."

"But you know what I mean," Jayson said. "I let myself get carried away trying to prove a point, and we lost a game we should have won."

"But now you get a chance to make things right," Mr. Lawton said. "It's one of the great things about sports: Sometimes you get a chance at redemption."

"I don't know much about redemption," Jayson said. "I just want a win."

The game in his old gym wasn't until four o'clock, a killer, the latest game they'd played all season. It turned out that the gym at Moreland East Middle was being used for a girls' basketball game first, so 'Cats vs. Mavs was going to be like the second game of a big basketball doubleheader.

It made him feel like he had another whole week to wait.

He ate breakfast, put on a hoodie and some sweatpants, went out and shot around on the Lawtons' court for what felt like an insanely long time. But when he finished and checked his phone, it was still only ten o'clock.

He went into the house and asked Mrs. Lawton if she'd mind driving him into town.

"Is there somewhere you need to be?" she said.

"Yeah, *somewhere,*" he said. "If I just hang around here for the next few hours, I'm gonna go crazy. I just want to wander around for a while."

She said if he wandered around until lunchtime, the two of them could grab a burger at the diner.

"Deal," Jayson said.

She dropped him off near the movie theater, and he told himself that if he just kept moving, he could make the time go faster. And maybe, just maybe, even though he hated all the waiting he still had to do, he could find a way to appreciate the anticipation he felt about finally getting to play this game.

So he just walked, up one street and down the other, keeping his head down, mostly, not wanting to run into anybody he knew. Telling himself, for around the thousandth time, that he wasn't going to make the same mistakes against his old team that he'd made the first time; telling himself that the Bobcats had won as a team ever since and would win as a team today. The only thing they were going to do today was prove that they were the better team now.

The next time he looked at his phone, a lot of time had actually passed. It was almost noon, and he felt himself getting hungry. He hit Mrs. Lawton up with a text, told her he was ready to take her up on that burger. She hit him back right away, saying she'd be there in fifteen minutes.

When he got to the diner, he looked through the front window, just to see how crowded it was.

That's when he saw Zoe.

She was in a booth in the front room, facing in his direction, and his first thought, despite his promise to stay focused only on the game, was that he was supposed to be here, that this was where they could finally have their talk.

Until he realized she wasn't alone.

She threw back her head and laughed at something the person facing her had just said. And Jayson wasn't surprised when that person turned out to be Eric Kelly.

The girl Jayson knew he still wanted to be with hadn't waited around for his explanation. She was with somebody else.

Jayson knew he should look away, knew how easy it would be for her to see him if she looked at the front window. But he was frozen to this spot. Just like he'd been in the supermarket that day.

He still didn't know much about girls, even if he knew a little more than he had before he'd moved to the west side. But he knew enough about Zoe Montgomery in that moment, seeing her sitting there laughing, seeing her with Eric, knowing that she was right where she was supposed to be, one soccer star hanging out with another. He could see how happy she looked, how comfortable. The two of them made sense.

He was about to move, to just walk up the street and wait for Mrs. Lawton, when Zoe locked eyes with him.

Eric was talking again, using his hands like he was trying to describe something to her. He was so busy he probably didn't even know that Zoe wasn't looking at him.

Didn't know she was looking straight at Jayson.

She didn't act surprised to see him there. Jayson knew he could be wrong, but he thought she looked a little sad, after having just looked so happy a minute before. It was almost like they *were* finally having a conversation with each other, the one that he'd been putting off. Like there weren't any more secrets between them now, just endless space.

The space he knew would always be there.

Finally she turned her attention back to Eric, and smiled. Jayson wondered later on if she took one more look back at him, out there on the street.

But Jayson was already gone.

WHEN THEY WERE INSIDE THE house, Jayson said he was going up to his room.

"You can talk to me about it, you know," Mrs. Lawton said. "Whatever happened today."

He thought about Zoe, pictured her smiling. Smiling with Eric Kelly. Should he have talked to her earlier, told her everything?

It didn't matter now. The moment was gone. It was almost as if he'd stolen from himself.

He felt as if he'd somehow let himself down today. He just wasn't sure why. He didn't know whether to be sad, or mad.

"Jayson? What is it?" Mrs. Lawton said.

"You're always so calm," Jayson said. "How do you do that?"

She laughed. "You don't know what kind of temper I *used* to have. Ever since I was a little girl."

"You?" He was genuinely surprised.

"Me."

"How did you get rid of it?"

"Years of practice," she said. "I worked at it. Almost as hard at it as you work on basketball."

"You grew up mad?"

"Furious. My anger could've melted the sun."

"What were you so mad about?"

"About being poor. About growing up without two parents in the house. Feeling stuck in the projects with no way to break out. A lot of the parts of my childhood made me so angry I wanted to scream. And I did. Often."

Maybe she did know more about what his life had been like than he'd given her credit for.

"Even these days, I feel my old attitude creeping back up on me when someone makes me mad, and I just want to shout and tell them that they don't know a darn thing about what's going on inside my head." She smiled and said, "But you wouldn't know anything about that, would you?"

"Little bit." He managed a smile, there and gone. In a snap.

"What happened today?"

And so he told her. All of it. Looking her in the eyes the whole time as he told her about what he'd heard from Mrs. Montgomery in the market that day; about why he'd really gone to the Jeff that day instead of meeting Zoe; about how he knew that he'd never be able to convince Zoe, no matter how hard he tried, that not everything her mom thought about him or had said about him was true.

And then he told her about seeing Zoe with Eric.

When he finished, the only sound in the room was the ticking of the kitchen clock.

Finally Mrs. Lawton said, "Jayson, it's not you who doesn't fit into Zoe's world. But if Zoe won't take the time to get to know you better, then maybe she doesn't fit into yours. And you know what? Her loss."

Jayson started to say something, but she put a finger to her lips. "I'm sure she's a very nice young girl, despite her narrow-minded mother. I'm sure she'll grow up to be a wonderful woman. But *you* are a great person, too, and no one should ever make you feel otherwise."

He wanted to thank her. But if he tried, he knew he wouldn't be able to stop the tears he felt coming on.

She smiled, though, as if she understood.

Then Carol Lawton said, "Life can be tough, Jayson, but you're even tougher. You can deal with anything thrown your way. Just remember that you don't have to handle it alone now. Not anymore."

Then Jayson was pushing back his chair, nearly knocking it over, coming around the table. Mrs. Lawton got up so he could come into her arms.

It was the first time in what felt like forever that he'd hugged someone.

35

GOING BACK TO THE GYM at Moreland East Middle was like going back to the Jeff. Today was going to feel like a road game that was really being played at home, against the only team in the league the Bobcats hadn't beaten this season.

Mrs. Lawton drove Jayson, Bryan, and Cameron to the game. All of Jayson's old boys were on the court by the time they got there around 3:30. The bleachers were already half full, Tyrese's mom and Shabazz's parents already in their seats.

The first thing Jayson did, just to get it out of the way, was go chest-bump some of his old teammates.

"C'mon, Snap, give us a smile," Tyrese said. "You know that game face of yours never scared me anyway."

"Just saying hi," Jayson said. "Talk to you after."

"Like we won't be talking during the game?" Ty said.

"One of us will," Jayson said. And he couldn't help but smile a little.

He walked over to say hello to Coach Rankin, who was standing at half-court.

"Go easy on us today," his old coach said.

Jayson grinned. "Trying to soften me up?"

"Depends. Is it working?"

"I know your moves as well as you know mine."

"Well, we're ready for you today," Coach said, grinning back at him. "How you doing over at Belmont? Everything good?"

"I miss playing for you, Coach, but I'm finally getting my groove back."

"I'm happy for you, Jayson. Good luck out there."

"Thanks, Coach. Same to you."

Jayson started to walk toward the home team's bench, old habit, but he stopped himself, and headed the other way.

In the huddle, the last thing Coach Rooney said to them was, "Enjoy the moment."

But then the moment seemed to swallow up just about everybody on the Bobcats except Jayson, his teammates starting this game the way they'd ended the last one against Geffen.

Cameron had three turnovers in the first quarter when he wasn't missing wide-open looks. At one point, Bryan threw two straight death passes in a row, floaters on the wing that got turned into easy breaks and easy baskets for the Mavs, one for Ty and one for Shabazz. The Bobcats were down 16–6 at the end of the first quarter, Jayson having scored all of his team's points.

Jayson really was ready to pop right now, feeling like he was the only one on the team who could step up and handle the pressure of the moment.

First Bobcat possession of the second quarter, he threw Cameron a perfect pass, straight at his chest, threading it through two defenders. All Cameron had to do was catch the ball to get himself an easy layup. Only he didn't catch the ball. Took his eyes off of it, started to shoot before he had even secured possession, and watched helplessly as it bounced off his hands and sailed out of bounds.

Jayson couldn't help himself.

"Come on, Cam! Get your head in the game!"

The words just came out of him. But somehow the gym had quieted down in that moment, and his voice bounced off the walls as if they'd put it out over the sound system.

As Jayson ran past the Bobcats' bench, Coach Rooney looked at him hard and said, "Dial it down, son."

On defense, Jayson was all over Ty, had been all game. Ty was 0 for 4 from the floor thus far, his shot seeming off by just a hair—the only part of the Mavs' game not working. So with Jayson once again playing him tight, Ty eventually gave up the ball to Shabazz, who looked to his right and spotted a wide-open Ray Bretton on the wing. No one was within ten feet of him. He squared up and calmly sank one of his sweet jumpers, a smile on his face as he let it go.

Jayson reacted instantly, looking around for Rashard. "You can't leave him open!" he shouted. "Ever!"

Coach, glaring now, said, “I’m not going to tell you again, Jayson. Dial it down. We’re all doing our best out there.”

“If that’s his best, then it’s not good enough!”

“That’s it. You’re done,” Coach said. “Take a seat.” He turned to the bench. “Alex, you’re in for Jayson.”

Jayson wheeled around at him. “You’re really gonna take me *out*?”

Coach came over, put a hand on his shoulder. “I am,” he said. “I’m your coach and I decide who plays and who sits. And if you don’t lower your voice and go sit down right away, I will send you out of this gym altogether. Now go sit.”

Humiliated, he walked past his teammates on the bench, sitting down as far away from Coach as he could. From there he watched the rest of the half, like there was an invisible wall separating him from the rest of his team.

To the rest of the team’s credit, Belmont hung in without Jayson. Down by thirteen when Jayson took the bench, the rest of the guys woke up and gave it their all.

With Jayson out, the offense ran through Cameron. Maybe it was Jayson leaving the game that did it; maybe Cam knew that someone had to step up and take charge—whatever the reason, he *finally* loosened up and started playing like his normal self. After a give-and-go from Bryan, Cameron sank a soft turnaround jumper right in front of the foul line.

Just getting that first basket was huge for Cam. For all of the Bobcats, really.

Alex Ahmad, given his first minutes all day, was full of energy. It helped that he was going up against Tyrese, who still couldn't buy a basket and who let down his guard just a little knowing that Jayson was on the bench. But the Mavericks kept putting the ball in Ty's hands, hoping to get their biggest scorer going. After a quick pass to Shabazz that was designed to get Ty an open look on the run, Alex timed the return pass perfectly. He jumped in front, knocking the ball away, then scrambled to get to it. With the team in transition, Alex then led Bryan just right with a bounce pass. Bryan pulled up, faked a jumper, and hit Cameron with a pass right in front of the basket. Two scores in a row for Cam.

Jayson couldn't believe that these were the same Bobcats who seemed lost on the court just minutes earlier.

From there, the 'Cats played with heart and purpose—and a ton of game—cutting into the Mavs' lead, one possession at a time.

When the horn sounded at the end of the half, the score was Mavericks 28, Bobcats 22. As the players filed into the locker room, Coach put a hand on Jayson's shoulder. Jayson turned around.

"You and I are going to take a walk. *Now.*" Coach's voice wasn't much louder than a whisper. But when Jayson looked at his face, he could see that Coach was still angry at him.

They walked out the double doors and past the boys' and girls' locker rooms, into the empty cafeteria.

Just the two of them. Coach motioned for Jayson to take a seat across from him at one of the round tables.

"By now you know that I always do what I say I'm gonna do, right?" Coach said.

"Right."

"Well," he said, "if you yell at one of your teammates again, I am going to sit you down for the rest of the game."

He was still talking in that quiet voice. But Jayson could see him fighting to control his own anger.

Coach said, "Is that clear?"

"Yes, sir."

"Look at me when you talk to me, son."

"Yes, sir," Jayson said, meeting his eyes.

"I don't care how well you're playing, or how good a player you are in general," Coach Rooney said. "If you're not a good teammate, if you bully your own guys, then you can't play on this team. I'll bench you, plain and simple. Is *that* understood?"

"Yes, sir."

"This is the way you acted at the very start of the season. I thought that was all in the past. Is there something bothering you that I should know about?"

The image of Zoe and Eric was in Jayson's head, there and gone. But all he did was shake his head, telling himself that Zoe Montgomery didn't matter right now. The only thing he cared about was beating his old team, winning the championship of this league.

"The only thing bothering me is the scoreboard."

"Well, you can't change it all by yourself," Coach said. "When we get back on that court, you do what you're supposed to do, and make everybody better."

Jayson nodded.

"Good." Coach managed a smile. "Now, go and show the Mavericks *exactly* what they're missing."

The second half played out much like the close of the first, with both teams going on mini-runs, but for the most part playing even ball. Jayson was now sharing the scoring load with Cam and Bryan, the way he had most of the season. Defensively, he continued to make life miserable for Ty, but Shabazz and Ray picked up the slack.

The Bobcats finished the third quarter on a 6–0 run to pull within two of the Mavs—by Jayson's count the fifth time they had been within two points. But not once had they been able to completely close the gap.

And it was about to get harder. On the first possession of the fourth quarter, two things happened at once that changed the whole complexion of the game.

Shabazz, still hoping to get Ty involved in the offense, passed up a shot and fed Ty in the corner. Ty launched a jumper, with Jayson all over him. As they came down, Ty landed on Jayson's foot, causing his ankle to turn. Jayson went down in a heap. The ball, meanwhile, found nothing but net.

Ty pumped his fist, barely even noticing Jayson on the ground, then leaped up and let out a shout. "THAT'S what I'm talking 'bout!"

As the Mavs chest-bumped Ty, the Bobcats surrounded Jayson, who was lying in pain on the court.

Coach Rooney called a time-out. "How bad is it, son?" he asked.

Jayson's ankle felt like it was on fire, but there was no way he was going to tell that to Coach. "Not bad. I just need to walk it off."

Moreland East's school physician arrived and unlaced Jayson's Zoom. He tested the ankle's range of motion and kept an eye on Jayson's face for reactions. Jayson was able to keep his cool. After a moment, the doctor said, "There's very little swelling. That's a good sign. Probably just a grade-one sprain. We should get it wrapped up, though, right away."

Cam offered Jayson a hand and helped him stand up. Jayson winced at the pressure on his ankle.

"Walk on it if you can," Coach said. "It's the only way to keep it loose."

Jayson was surprised that he actually did feel better walking on it.

He went to the bench and sat as the ankle was wrapped up tight. He looked downcourt and caught Ty's eye. Ty seemed to be asking him a question without saying a word.

Jayson nodded, and Ty gave a small smile of relief before nodding back.

Then Jayson was up on his feet and ready to go. He had no idea how long he could last on the ankle. But he was about to find out. They all were at Moreland East.

It wasn't long before Jayson discovered two things. First, he could handle the pain. Second, the ankle wrap was stealing his quick first step. The player who had been nicknamed Snap for the way he could disappear in a flash was now hobbling just enough to rob him of his speed. With Ty finally having found his shot, this was not a good combination. Jayson knew his friend would be coming fast now, calling for the ball, looking for his shot every trip down the court. If Jayson couldn't keep up with him, he'd be doing more harm than good for the 'Cats.

Midway through the fourth, Jayson was beginning to feel the pain again. All the planting and quick changes of direction were tough on the ankle. Ty hadn't shown him any mercy, driving past him twice for buckets, and faking a third time before pulling up to sink a sweet jumper.

"You sure you don't want to just give us the game now and save yourself some heartbreak?" Ty asked him after the jumper.

"Keep talking, Ty," Jayson said. "It's the best game you got going."

Offensively, Jayson was having trouble driving the ball east and west, missing with his own jumper. But he kept finding the open man every chance he got. Between Cam, Bryan, and a big-time three from Rashard, Belmont stayed in the game. But Ty was killing them whenever he had the ball.

A minute and forty-seven seconds left. Mavs by seven, their ball. Jayson was feeling every step by now, his legs tired from having to take pressure off the ankle. Coach had noticed, so he subbed in Alex.

"Don't sit," Coach said to Jayson. "Don't want that ankle tightening up on you. Just take a breather."

"I'm fine, Coach. Don't need a breather."

"A shame, because you're getting one. Let Alex do his thing and we'll get you back out there for the finish."

Alex doing his thing was using his fresh legs to harass Ty. Ty wasn't about to back down from the challenge, Jayson knew. If anything, it would only make Ty want the ball more. Alex was two inches shorter than Jayson, and Ty saw any height advantage as the perfect excuse to shoot more jumpers. It was who he was. Who he'd always been.

Jayson told this to Coach Rooney, who quickly called out a play to his guys on the floor.

And as soon as Ty had the ball in his hands, Cam stepped out of the paint and threw a hand up to challenge the shot. Ty had to adjust midshot and it was just enough to alter the trajectory of the ball, which bounced high off the far side of the hoop, out of the reach of Shabazz, before landing in Bryan's hands.

Cam, already clear of the paint, headed downcourt at full sprint. Bryan saw him and threw a high, arcing pass that landed right in Cam's hands, with no one between him and the basket.

Mavs by five now.

Once again, Ty called for the ball and found himself isolated against Alex. Cam separated himself from Shabazz, ready to sprint out to help. Ty saw it and jumped. Only this time he threw a perfect pass to Shabazz, right in front of the net. An easy two for Moreland East.

Ty turned and wagged his finger at Jayson, a grin wide on his face. Talking trash without saying a word.

It was here that Coach told Jayson to go in for Alex on the next whistle. "We can't afford to just trade baskets," he said to Jayson. "Someone needs to step up and get us some stops."

Jayson's legs felt less wobbly after the brief rest. He dribbled slowly, letting the players get their positions, Ty giving him some space, practically daring Jayson to drive to the lane. Instead, Jayson took advantage of the good look he got and launched a three-pointer right over Ty's outstretched hand. Nothing but net. The lead came down to four with under a minute left.

Coach Rooney told the Bobcats not to foul.

The Mavs took their time heading down the floor, using up clock. Jayson focused on Ty, looking to make a steal. Ty passed to Ray, who'd had a hot first half but had gone cold in the second. Ray saw Shabazz angling against Cam, looking for the ball, so he fed him. Shabazz dribbled once, faked going left, then left his feet for a turnaround jumper.

Cam didn't buy the fake. Careful not to foul, he kept his eyes on the ball and reached out a long arm, his fingertips just getting a piece of the shot. The ball spun straight up. Cam and Shabazz both jumped for it; Cam's hand got there first. He swatted the ball off the backboard, where it landed right in Rashard's hands.

Rashard found Jayson and passed him the ball. This time, Ty played Jayson a little tighter. Jayson wasn't about to launch another three, though. Down by four with thirty-eight seconds left, Jayson knew it was a two-possession lead. He checked Cam's position against Shabazz, then glanced toward Bryan. The two locked eyes for just a second. Jayson liked what he saw and fired off a pass. Bryan faked pulling up, getting Ray into the air. Then he drove right past, into the lane. Shabazz left Cam to challenge the shot, but Bryan waited for the contact before releasing the ball—a perfect teardrop off the glass, with a foul shot to follow.

Bryan wheeled and found Jayson. "No fear," he said with a smile.

Jayson bumped him some fist. "No fear. Now knock this down and bring us to one."

It was exactly what Bryan did.

Thirty-six seconds left. Just enough so that the thirty-five-second shot clock was still in play. Moreland East couldn't run out the clock. But everyone knew they would milk it as much as they could, setting up what they hoped would be their last basket.

The Mavs spread the court, keeping the ball moving. Ty to Ray to Paul Henderson. In to Shabazz. Right back out to Paul. The seconds ticking down, the ball being passed like a game of keep-away.

Jayson knew something, though. He knew where that ball would eventually end up when Moreland East ran out of time to waste and had to shoot.

Sure enough, with ten seconds left on the shot clock, the ball went to Ty, who had no intention of letting it go again.

The game seemed to slow down for Jayson at that point. He pictured the move he wanted to make, saw himself making it, even on one good leg. Not giving anything away. Concentrating only on the body in front of him, the rhythm of the ball. Not moving an inch, making Ty think he was in total control.

Wait for it.

Shot clock down to five, the game clock to six.

Ty crouched just a little, dribbled the ball just a little harder, ready to make his move. *Now.*

Jayson flicked out a hand.

Knocked the ball away.

Now was when he needed just one last burst, that first step his ankle hadn't been allowing him. Jayson reached the loose ball one step ahead of Ty and took off.

Kept going all the way to the hoop, where he laid the ball in.

Horn sounded.

Final. Belmont 57, Moreland East 56.

JAYSON WAS IN THE FRONT seat of Mrs. Lawton's parked car. "You're absolutely sure you don't want me to go in with you?"

"I'm sure. As much as I appreciate everything you and Mr. Lawton have done for me, this is something I *have* to do by myself."

He got out of the car, stopped briefly on the sidewalk, took a deep breath and then another, and walked through the front door and into the Foot Locker in Percy.

It wasn't nearly as crowded on a weekday afternoon as it had been the day he had come here by himself, the day he'd done a bad thing that ended up changing his life. At first, he'd fought those changes, *hard*, determined to stay in control of his life. But now he had people who cared about him, Mrs. and Mr. Lawton, Ms. Moretti, his coach, and his friends. He still was in control of things, but now he had some help along the way, didn't have to worry about doing everything on his own anymore.

He had called the store before they made the drive over

here, and the girl who answered had told him, yes, Pete was working today.

Jayson looked around, but didn't spot him right away; all he saw was a few young guys and girls in their referee shirts helping customers try on sneakers.

He looked in the other direction. Still no sight of him. In a minute he'd ask somebody to go find him. For now he walked over to the display of Zooms.

The blue-and-white Zooms that Jayson had worn this season were sitting up on the shelf, just like they had been that day a few months back.

"I can't decide," he heard a voice next to him say.

He turned and saw a boy who was just slightly smaller than him staring up at all the basketball shoes.

Jayson immediately looked down to see that the kid was wearing a pair of old, scuffed-up Adidas high-tops.

"Sorry?" Jayson said.

"My mom said I could use my birthday money from my grandparents to buy new sneakers," the kid said. "But I can't decide."

"What's your favorite team?"

"Duke," the boy said. "The Blue Devils."

"Then check out the blue-and-white Zooms," Jayson said, pointing. "I've got the same ones."

The boy reached up, pulled the display sneakers off the wall, and said he'd be right back. He wanted to show his mom.

It was then that Jayson turned around and saw Pete staring at him.

Maybe even remembering what had happened the last time Jayson was here.

But then the moment was there and gone, because the boy was back with his mother. He walked in front of Jayson's eyeline, telling one of the Foot Locker employees that he knew his size, he'd made up his mind, these were the ones he had to have.

"Thank you!" the boy said, sitting down on the bench to wait. "They're perfect."

Jayson walked over to where Pete was standing.

He had most of the money he had saved up since buying the Christmas horse for Mrs. Lawton in his pocket, the $130 in cash he knew he needed for the sneakers he'd stolen.

He took the wad of cash out of his pocket and handed it to Pete.

"You don't owe anything," Pete said. "Mr. Lawton made good on them a while ago."

"I know," Jayson said. "But *I* didn't make good on what I did. Maybe you can just keep the money and buy a pair for somebody who can't afford new kicks."

Pete looked at him and nodded. "Okay, then." He shook Jayson's hand.

Jayson was on his way out of the store when he felt Pete's hand on his shoulder. But today, Pete's grip was lighter.

This time, Jayson wasn't trapped.

He turned around to look at Pete.

"Good luck in the championship game," Pete said.

"Thank you."

Jayson walked out the door of the Foot Locker. This time, he left with his head held high, finally not looking over his shoulder.

HOW DID HE END UP here?

Jayson felt like he was watching some kind of movie, with a bunch of twists and turns, almost like he was a spectator to everything that had happened, and was still happening, in front of his eyes.

Ms. Moretti and Mrs. Lawton were always telling him that the journey was as important as the destination, and he knew what they were saying. But still:

He was here.

He'd made it to Cameron.

They all had, because they'd won their game against Moreland East, because they'd led the Percy Hawks from start to finish in the league championship game, more of a team that day than they'd ever been. They'd grown together. Grown *up* together. And had learned to trust each other.

Now, in a couple of minutes, they would go out and play the state middle-grade championship against the team from Raleigh.

They were here.

The Bobcats had won a coin flip, so they were the ones who'd gotten to dress in the Duke locker room tonight. By now, over the three days and nights they'd been in Durham, they'd seen most of Cameron Indoor Stadium, Jayson surprised at how much smaller it was than he'd thought it would be. But maybe things were always bigger in your dreams.

So much of it reminded Jayson of some old-fashioned gym, right down to the concession stands, and the way they rolled out bleachers for games, and even the fake, tall doors up at the top of the place.

They'd looked up at all the NCAA championship banners and ACC banners and even one that said, "Southern Conference 1938." They'd sat where the Cameron Crazies sat in the student section, and in the soft blue seats that were right behind the two team benches.

"Like they can reach out and touch the game," Bryan had said, more excited than Jayson had ever seen him, more full of nervous energy.

But then they all were, even Coach.

In the locker room, they'd taken pictures of each other in front of the four Duke NCAA championship plaques, and in the coaches' conference room with the huge TV screen in there. They'd sat and posed and mugged on the couches in the players' lounges. Jayson had made sure to have Bryan take a picture of him in front of a picture of Bobby Hurley, the great Duke point guard who'd helped the Blue Devils win two national championships. Even though Hurley played before

Jayson was born, long before he was born, Jayson knew about him. Every point guard in North Carolina did, he was pretty sure.

"Long way for me from the Jeff," Jayson said to Bryan now.

"Long way from anywhere," Bryan said. Then he said, "Ankle still good?"

"Perfect," Jayson said.

Everything felt that way tonight.

Along with the rest of the 'Cats, they were standing in what was called the Defensive Room, off the locker room, pictures on the walls in here of all the Duke players who had ever won Defensive Player of the Year.

"If the last thing Coach K wants his players to be thinking about is defense before they take the court," Coach Rooney said, keeping his voice low, "that's good enough for me."

He turned to Jayson then and said, "You ready?"

Jayson grinned. "What do you think?"

Then he was the first to do what they'd been told Duke players did before they ran out of here to play the game: He leaned down and slapped the most famous "D" in basketball, the Duke logo, at his feet.

Then Bryan did the same, and Cameron, and Brandon, and Marty and Alex Ahmad. Jayson watched them, thinking he had one kind of family now with the Lawtons. But this was his other family. His team. Cameron Indoor had been the goal from the start. But being on this team? That was where he really belonged, it had just taken him a while to figure it out.

In the small, quiet room, like a waiting room before the title game, the slaps sounded as loud as firecrackers going off.

Yeah, Jayson thought.

Long way from the Jeff.

"Lead us out, Jayson," Coach Rooney said.

He walked over and opened the door. He ran out and then they all did, down the long hallway and into all the noise and light of Cameron Indoor Stadium, not running away from anything anymore, just into the rest of his life.

Turn the page for a preview of

Mike Lupica's

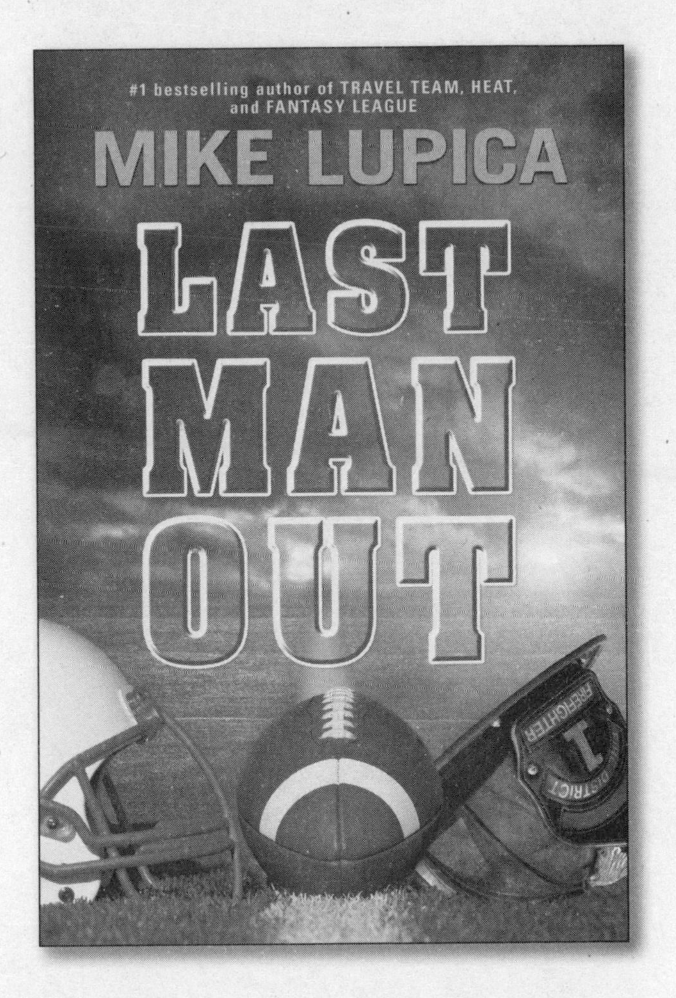

ONE

AS USUAL, HE WAS JUST RUNNING around looking for people to hit.

Not in a dirty way that might get somebody on the other team hurt, or get himself hurt. Tommy Gallagher wasn't that type of football player. That wasn't him. More importantly, that wasn't how his dad had taught him to play the game.

"Always remember that cheap shots are called that for a reason," Patrick Gallagher reminded Tommy before the season started, as if Tommy needed reminding. "You throw one of those, you're the one who ends up looking cheap. You don't lay out a guy who's defenseless, you don't take out a guy's knees, and you never go looking to put your hat on the other guy's."

That was what Patrick Gallagher called helmets: hats.

"Lead with my shoulder," Tommy said.

"And your great big oversized heart," his dad said.

Tommy was leading with both today. His official position with the Brighton Bears was strong safety. But his dad said that he was really what they used to call a "monster back" in his day, just like the retired Pittsburgh Steeler Troy Polamalu. The great defender known for his big plays and big head of hair. Tommy played like him, which meant he was a safety and linebacker and baseball center fielder all at once.

And a hitter.

Tommy's coach, John Fisher, liked to tell people, "Tommy Gallagher's real position is wherever the football happens to be at a given moment."

Patrick Gallagher put it another way: He said Tommy found the fastest route to the ball the way the GPS in your car found you the fastest way home.

Tommy had been doing that all morning against the Allston Jaguars. Playing in the Bears' second game of the season, he'd been racking up stats and hits. He'd already intercepted his first pass of the year. He'd forced two fumbles, recovering one himself. He'd broken up pass play after pass play and had absolutely shut down the Jaguars' running game, even beating defensive linemen and linebackers to the ball all the way from the secondary. And that was no easy thing considering the Bears' middle linebacker Rob Greco—known as "Greck," the way the Patriots' tight end Rob Gronkowski was known as "Gronk"—was a heat-seeking missile on a football field.

But Tommy was having that kind of day, flying around the field from the moment the ball had been kicked off. Now it was third and ten from midfield, and when he looked over at Coach John Fisher on the sideline, Tommy was happy to see him signal for a blitz. For Tommy, there was nothing more fun in football than getting to the quarterback.

He timed the snap count perfectly, blew past the Jags' left

offensive tackle, then shoved the running back trying to block him out of the way. Now he had a clear path to the Jags' quarterback, Ryan Combs. Ryan was looking to his right as he started to set himself to throw, locked in on his receiver. He had no idea that Tommy, coming from his blind side, had a clear shot at him. But Tommy didn't take the shot, because Ryan was defenseless in that moment. That would've been the *definition* of a cheap shot. Instead, Tommy wrapped Ryan up in a bear hug, then put him down on the ground.

It was a full sack. But only half a hit from Tommy Gallagher, though his teammates said that even half a hit from him was bad enough.

When the play was over, Tommy reached down and helped Ryan, a good guy he knew from summer camp, get back up on his feet.

"Are you sure you're not lining up in our backfield?" Ryan said after he handed the ball to the ref.

"That would take all the fun out of it."

"I'm sorry," Ryan said. "This is *fun*?"

Tommy grinned. "For me it is."

"Is there any chance you could dial down the fun factor a little bit?"

"Well, I could," Tommy said. "But I'd have to find another sport."

Ryan tipped his helmet back so Tommy could see he was grinning, too.

"I'm willing to help you with that!" he said.

The Jags' punt team was coming onto the field. Ryan jogged

toward his bench, while Greck and Tommy ran toward their own.

"Dude, I can't believe you beat me to the quarterback again!" Greck said. "You are totally on fire today."

As soon as he said it, Greck realized his mistake. Everybody on the team knew that Tommy didn't like anybody using that word around him.

Fire.

Patrick Gallagher, Tommy's dad, was a Boston fireman. One of Boston's bravest. Tommy knew that fire was part of his dad's job—no, it *was* his job—but that didn't mean he had to like it. He loved the idea that his dad sometimes saved lives. He understood the risks his dad had to take, even though Patrick Gallagher liked to joke he was in more danger turning on the grill in the backyard than he was on the job.

As much as his dad joked around, though, Tommy knew his dad put his life on the line every day on the job. So Tommy still didn't want to be talking about fire when he was playing football. Or thinking about it.

"Sorry," Greck said.

"Hey, no worries," Tommy said, slapping Greck on the shoulder pads.

Even at twelve, Tommy understood that his dad put his life in danger for the job. He knew what a difference his dad made in people's lives. As important as football was to Tommy—and his dad—though, he would never treat football like a life-or-death situation.

All I'm trying to do, Tommy thought, is make plays, win football games, and have fun doing it.

There was plenty of fun going around today. But the Bears were still only leading the Jags 12–7, midway through the third quarter. The Bears' quarterback and one of Tommy's best friends on the team, Nick Petty, had thrown two touchdown passes in the first quarter. But their offense had produced nothing since, and one of the Jags' wide receivers had returned a punt for a touchdown right before halftime. And it didn't help that the Bears had missed both extra-point attempts. So even though Tommy and Greck and the rest of the guys on defense were piling on the hits, the game was way too close with a lot of time left on the clock.

Tommy ran right up to Nick while the Jags' punter was kicking the ball out of bounds.

"Get me some points," Tommy said.

"Trying," Nick said. Then he poked Tommy with an elbow as he said, "You're saying we don't have enough already to win?"

"We do," Tommy said. "I just want you to be able to relax a little in the fourth."

"With you around?" Nick said. "No shot. Coach goes easier on me than you do."

"Get me more points."

"You said that already," Nick said. "And I told you I'm trying."

Tommy gave Nick a little shove toward the field. "Like my dad always says, trying is good but doing is better."

Speaking of his dad, Tommy looked into the stands, hoping to spot him. No luck.

Patrick Gallagher, filling in for a friend, was supposed to get off his overnight shift at eleven o'clock. Tommy never looked at his phone during a game, but he figured it had to be well past eleven by now because the game had started at ten. Tommy turned his head and took another look at the bleachers behind their bench. His dad wasn't in his usual spot, alone in the corner of the last row, where he always was, wherever the game was being played, home or away. His mom usually sat with the other moms, which she was doing today, his sister, Emily, right beside her. But when his dad got here, Tommy knew he'd head right to the top corner. He liked to be able to concentrate, without any distractions, on every move Tommy made. Good or bad. Win or lose.

Tommy always heard about the highs and the lows when they got together after the game.

On the next drive, Nick and the offense didn't get him more points, didn't even get a first down, or give the defense much of a breather. So Tommy was back out there before he knew it. But after what felt like a minute later, he was batting away a third-down pass intended for the Jags' tight end. He was off the field just as quickly as he'd gotten back on it. If the Bears weren't going to score more points, neither were the Jags. If it meant that Tommy had to do whatever it took to make Brighton's lead stand up, fine with him. In a close game like this, there was always a part of him, a big one, that made him feel as if the game were in his hands as much as Nick's.

Maybe more.

It was still 12–7 four minutes into the fourth quarter and the Jags were on their best drive of the game. Ryan was mixing up runs and passes, managing for these few minutes to run away from Tommy and make quick throws to the outside that negated

Tommy's speed and instincts. Then Greck made a rare mistake, letting the Jags' tight end get behind him on the left sideline. Tommy could only watch helplessly from the middle of the field as Ryan made a sweet throw, hitting his receiver in stride. As he did, Tommy was already at full speed, trying to get back into the play, finally catching the kid from behind and bringing him down at the Bears' ten-yard line.

Game on.

"I'm an idiot!" Greck said in the huddle, banging the sides of his helmet with his huge hands.

"Everyone makes mistakes," Tommy said. "But you're still a great football player."

"Not on that play."

"What play?" Tommy said. "I don't remember that one."

It was another thing Patrick Gallagher always talked about: developing instant amnesia about a play that had already happened.

"I hear you," Greck said, nodding. "I got this."

"No," Tommy said. "*We* got this."

On the next play, the Jags' running back ran up the middle for four yards, Tommy and Greck combining on the tackle. Ryan tried to fool them on second down, rolling to his right like he was planning to keep it himself and run. But Tommy read the play perfectly, read the *blockers* perfectly, and saw that they were running laterally without crossing the line of scrimmage.

Pass.

Out of the corner of his eye, he saw one of the Jags' wide receivers coming from the other side of the field, running easily, as if he weren't really in on the play. But Tommy knew better, and immediately revised what he'd just said to Greck in the huddle.

I got this, he told himself.

At the exact same moment Ryan pulled up to pass, eyes locked on his target, seeing him wide open in the middle of the field, but not seeing Tommy at all. Tommy was ready, breaking hard toward the wide receiver just as Ryan released the ball.

It all happened fast, like a video replay that's been sped up ten times. It happened the way it had when the Patriots had beaten the Seahawks in the last seconds of Super Bowl XLIX, when Patriots' defensive back Malcolm Butler had read Seahawks' quarterback Russell Wilson perfectly right before stepping in and making the most famous interception in Super Bowl history.

Tommy was the one reading the play now in Allston, running along the goal line, cutting in front of the receiver as Ryan's pass arrived.

Finding the fastest route to the ball one more time.

It turned out to be a perfect throw. Only problem for the Jags was that it landed right in Tommy's hands.

He heard the intended receiver yell "Hey!" as Tommy caught the ball, running toward the sideline, already picking up speed as the rest of the players seemed to be going in the other direction, not realizing that offense had suddenly become defense. Tommy tucked the ball under his right arm and had plenty of time and room to turn himself upfield, with all that open space ahead of him, all that green.

He gave a quick look over his left shoulder and saw some white Jaguar jerseys starting to give chase. The Allston players must've realized what happened, how quickly the play had turned around, maybe wondering how Tommy had gotten to midfield this fast. His quick, long strides brought him closer and closer to the end zone. Forty-yard line now.

Thirty.

Try and catch me.

Tommy could feel himself smiling. He thought about taking another look back to see if any defenders were close behind. But there was no need. He had kicked it up to high gear and he was only racing against himself now.

Twenty.

Ten.

He was crossing into the end zone when he heard the siren.

TRAVEL TEAM

Danny may be the smallest kid on the basketball court, but no one has a bigger love of the game. When the local travel team cuts Danny because of his size, he's determined to show just how strong he can be. It turns out he's not the only kid who was cut for the wrong reasons. Now Danny is about to give all the castoffs a second chance and prove that you can't measure heart.

SUMMER BALL

Leading your travel team to the national championship may seem like a dream come true, but for Danny, being at the top just means the competition tries that much harder to knock him down. Now Danny's heading to basketball camp for the summer with all the country's best players in attendance. But old rivals and new battles leave Danny wondering if he really does have what it takes.

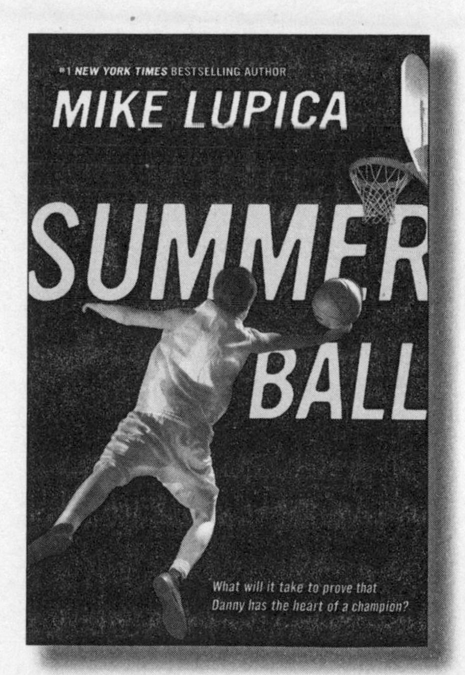

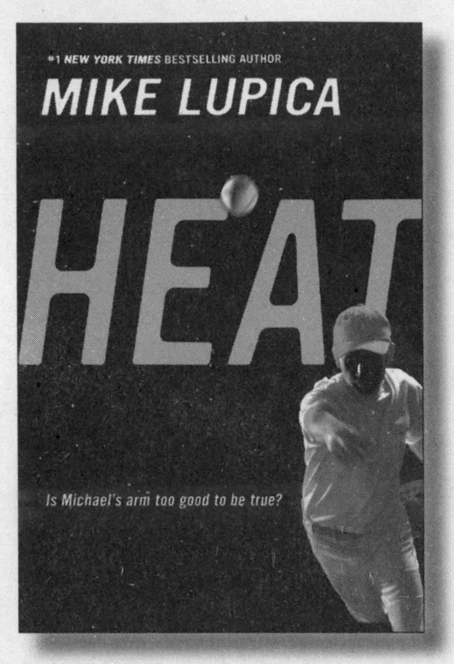

HEAT

Michael has a pitching arm that throws serious heat. But his firepower is nothing compared to the heat he faces in his day-to-day life. Newly orphaned after his father led the family's escape from Cuba, Michael carries on with only his seventeen-year-old brother. But then someone discovers Michael's talent, and his secret world is blown wide-open.

MIRACLE ON 49TH STREET

Josh Cameron is MVP of the championship Boston Celtics. When twelve-year-old Molly arrives in his life, claiming to be his daughter, she catches him off guard. But as Molly gets to know the real Josh, she starts to understand why her mother kept her from him for so long. Josh has room in his heart for only two things: basketball and himself.

THE BIG FIELD

Playing shortstop is a way of life for Hutch—which is why having to play second base feels like a demotion. But Hutch is willing to stand aside if it's best for the team, even if it means playing in the shadow of Darryl, the best shortstop prospect since A-Rod. But with the league championship on the line, just how far is Hutch willing to bend to be a good teammate?

THE BATBOY

Brian is a batboy for his hometown major-league team and believes it's the perfect thing to bring him and his big-leaguer dad closer together. This is also the season that Brian's baseball hero, Hank Bishop, returns to the Tigers for the comeback of a lifetime. But when Hank Bishop starts to show his true colors, Brian learns that sometimes life throws you a curveball.

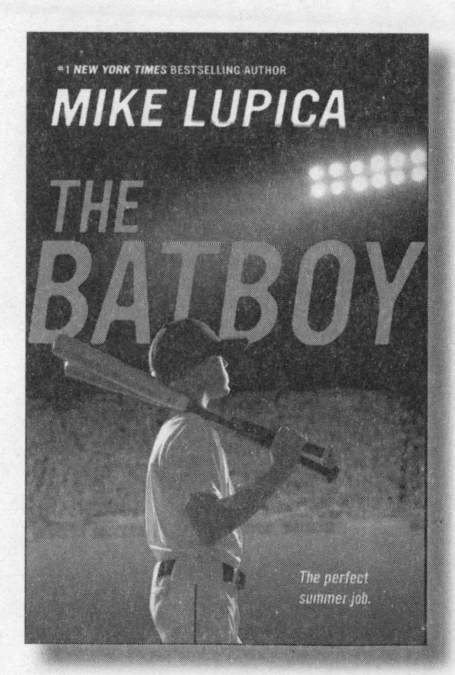

MILLION-DOLLAR THROW

Everyone calls Nate Brodie "Brady" because he's a quarterback, just like his idol, Tom Brady, and is almost as good. Now he's won a chance to win a million dollars by throwing one pass through a target at halftime of a pro game. The pressure is more than he can bear, and suddenly the golden boy is having trouble completing a pass . . . but can he make the one that really counts?

THE UNDERDOGS

Will is about the fastest thing on two legs in Forbes, Pennsylvania. On the football field, no one can stop him. But when his town experiences a financial crisis, putting many of its residents out of work, it's up to Will to lift the town's spirits by giving everyone something to cheer about.

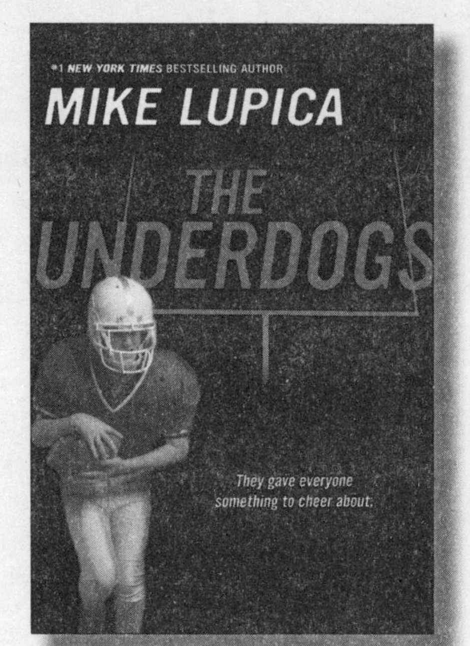

HERO

Zach thought he knew his dad—former football star, special adviser to the president. But then Zach's father's plane crashes under mysterious circumstances. Now Zach is left without a clue of who *he* really is: a fourteen-year-old superhero.

TRUE LEGEND

For basketball phenom Drew Robinson, there is nothing more true than his talent on the court. It's the kind that comes along once in a generation and is loaded with perks—and with problems. Before long, True begins to buy in to his own hype—and suddenly trouble has a way of finding him. That is, until a washed-up former playground legend steps back onto the court and takes True under his wing.

QB 1

Jake Cullen lives in a Texas-sized shadow. His father is a local football legend who made it in the NFL, and his older brother is a can't-miss QB prospect who led the varsity team to the state title last season. Now the bright lights of Texas high school football shine on freshman Jake. Trouble is, Jake is in no hurry to live in the shadow of his famous family.

FANTASY LEAGUE

Charlie may be just a bench warmer for his school's football team, but when it comes to knowing all the stats and loving the game, he's one of the best. And when a sports radio host plays Charlie's fantasy picks on air, he becomes a celebrity and personal friend of the owner of the L.A. Bulldogs. But soon he comes to realize that living the dream and confronting the reality of his decisions are very different things.